HIDDEN IN THE CAPITOL

B. IVY WOODS

BRETAGEY PRESS

To Chelsie,

Thank you for reading every thing that I write and for being one of
my biggest supporters.

1

———

A FEW MONTHS AGO

"This has to be kept quiet."

Evelyn "Eve" Jackson's ears perked up at what sounded like a woman's voice. The voice interrupted the reminders she was trying to create for herself after the congressional interview she conducted that day. She was walking back through the underground tunnels in the basement of Cannon House Office Building toward Longworth to where she had luckily scored a parking spot not too far from the Capitol. She slowed to a stop and strained to listen to the words spoken by a woman just around the corner. Normally she tried to mind her own business unless it was a story she was pursuing, because what better way to stay out of trouble? This time though, the urgency in the woman's voice caught Eve by surprise. Who was she? Was she talking to someone on the phone or was this person with her? Was security still there? Were these people talking freely in front of them?

"Don't you think I know that? No one will breathe a word of this, I promise you." Eve's question was answered when a smooth Southern drawl responded to the woman's plea. She could hear the couple coming closer and decided her best course of action was to move back a couple of steps so she could still be within earshot, yet hopefully somewhat out of sight. She turned around and saw a cleaning cart. Eve had seconds to form and execute a plan. Her shoulders almost touched her ears when her shoes squeaked on the floor as she darted behind the cart, her mind unable to figure out how loud the noise was. Had the man and woman a few feet away heard or seen her before she reached the cart? She peered out and her shoulders relaxed as the man and woman came into view. They didn't suspect a thing. It was two people having a conversation, just as she had suspected.

Eve squinted her eyes to get a better look at the couple. She could see only their profiles, but the woman looked familiar. The woman's hair appeared auburn under the glow of the lights and was haphazardly thrown over one shoulder. She ran her hands through her shoulder-length hair, further disheveling it before she smoothed her hands down her dark green dress. The man next to her had perfectly styled blond hair, longer on top, and a well-fitted dark suit. When the woman turned her head in Eve's direction, Eve ducked behind the cart. But she saw enough to identify the woman.

Kayla Harper was the communications director for Representative Anthony Blake. Eve interviewed the congressman about a month ago to talk about his reelection and what plans he had for the next year. They were entering the lame-duck session, which usually meant that few legislative items would get done while they prepared for the next congressional term.

She hoped the dark tunnel concealed her identity. She looked up and found a security camera above her head. Was it rolling and catching all of this? Eve peeped around the cleaning cart once more.

"This has the potential to ruin several lives." Mystery man looked down and fingered his tie.

"Don't you think I know that?" Eve couldn't see the expression on Kayla's face, but she noted the exasperation and quivering in her voice. "We need to figure out a way to keep this under wraps. After all, it's been a secret for years."

"True. This needs to stay buried in the Capitol."

Kayla nodded and glanced around before walking away. Mystery man walked in a different direction and Eve waited a beat before standing up from her crouched position and leaving her hiding spot. When she was a few feet away from where the couple once stood, a loud bang startled her. Eve swung around and saw a janitor standing near the cleaning cart that she had just left. He gave her a small wave and she smiled before turning her attention back to where Kayla and her associate once were. Eve gave another smile to the security guard who was seated across the room and headed toward Longworth, debating what she should do with the information she'd overheard.

But what she didn't know was that someone else was watching this entire episode unfold, deeper in the shadows. And it wasn't the security officer that she had just said goodnight to.

~

A FEW DAYS LATER, Eve was at the Green Hat waiting for Flint and Rae to arrive. They had wanted to get their friends and family together before the holidays. Eve thought this was a little weird, but maybe it was a last-minute smaller celebration for Flint's big win. Liv decorated the room for the holidays, although most of the decor items were gold and white. That included the balloons that surrounded the bar and the table where snacks and hors d'oeuvres were stationed.

She was standing in the corner with Jules as Liv was busy running around trying to make sure that everything was in place.

"Here are pictures from the fundraiser we held last night." Jules held her phone so Eve could see, and the two commented on some famous people they spotted in the photos.

"Looks like it was an outstanding event."

"Probably one of the best we've held to date."

Jules was still swiping through the photos when Eve felt the hairs on the back of her neck stand up. The air in the room changed drastically, alerting her that something was afoot. Eve knew he had arrived. She looked to her left and her gaze floated around the room until she reached him. There was no denying where his eyes were looking, or the warmth in them.

"Hey, Jules?"

"Yep?" Jules looked up from her phone.

"Can you hold my drink for a moment? I'm going to head to the bathroom."

"Yeah, sure, no problem," Jules said as she took the glass from Eve. Eve walked to the entrance of the private room that Flint and Rae had rented for their holiday celebration. She knew she would have to pass Kane to reach the bathroom. Just as she was closing in on the doorway, she glanced at him; he stared back at her. The warmth of his gaze had turned up several notches, but she refused to look away until absolutely necessary, because she had to look where she was going.

Her trip to the bathroom was quick and painless because there was no line and no one else was in there. As she washed her hands, she recalled flashes of what happened a few short months ago when she stood outside the bathroom and heard the confrontation between Rae and Cassandra. She shook the thoughts from her mind as she flicked droplets of water into the sink, trying to remove excess water from her hands before she headed over to grab a paper towel.

She tossed her head to the side, causing her short, dark brown strands to shift out of her eyes, and sighed. The mirror in front of her did nothing to hide the fact that she had bags under dark brown eyes from a lack of sleep. She would say that work had been keeping her up late, but it was more than that. The conversation she overheard ran on a loop through her mind.

Eve grabbed a paper towel, dried her hands and used the same paper towel to open the bathroom door before tossing it into the trash. She speed-walked back into the private party room, not stopping to see where Kane was or if he was still in the room. She found Jules, who was now joined by Liv, who was finally finished with party prep. The trio waited for the couple of the hour to arrive so they could ring in the holiday a little early.

Eve was still riding high from celebrating Rae and Flint's announcement. They were engaged! After about an hour and a half, the party seemed to be winding down although very few people had left. Eve stretched and checked her phone.

Her eyes widened as she questioned the message she was seeing. Her stomach dropped into the bowels of hell.

Eve,

Whatever you thought you heard was a misunderstanding. Forget it now, before it's too late.

The email was unsigned.

She reread the message three times before declaring that what she was seeing was real. Her eyes drifted up to find out who the email was from but instead found a series of letters before and after the @. Without a doubt, it was a spoof account. Almost no chance of her being able to find out who the sender was. That further cemented the worry in the pit of her stomach. She looked up and was thankful to see one of her best friends standing nearby.

"Rae?"

Rae swung around and their eyes connected.

"Hey, what's up?" Rae paused before she asked, "Is everything all right?"

Eve felt her hands shaking but could do nothing to control it. "I'm n-not sure. This was just sent to my work email." Rae scanned the email and almost dropped the phone.

"You've got to be shitting me."

When the two looked up, they found Kane staring back at them with an eyebrow raised.

Neither woman said anything as Eve turned her back to Kane to talk to Rae privately.

"Maybe it's a prank."

"Eve, does this sound like a prank to you?" Rae stared at

her friend in amazement. "Someone is trying to stop you from working on a story."

Eve sighed and ran a hand through her pixie cut, causing her hair to stand even more on edge. Her mind raced as she tried to come up with a reason for the email.

"Look, I shouldn't have brought this up. We're here to celebrate you and Flint, not talk about an email that I got."

"But your safety is important. Way more important than this surprise engagement party." Rae reached over to hug Eve and when she pulled away, she asked, "Are you treading on thin ice with an article you're working on?"

Eve took a deep breath and, just as she was about to respond, someone interrupted her.

"Is something wrong?"

Eve slowly turned around and faced the person who interrupted their conversation.

There stood Kane in all of his glory. Although Rae was standing there with Eve, Kane's hazel eyes were trained on Eve. His gaze held a low simmer that Eve could only imagine would grow more intense if he saw the email she received.

"There's nothing wrong. Even if there was, I wouldn't come to you."

Kane sighed. "I thought we'd moved on from what happened before, when I got you the press pass; you captured Cassandra confessing to Rae."

"That was to help Rae and Flint, not me personally."

"I—"

"Kane, everything is fine, okay? I can take care of all of this myself." Eve turned her attention back to her best friend and returned the hug Rae gave a few moments prior. "I'm going to head out, okay? I have a few things to finish up and I should probably get home. I'm so happy for you and Flint. I'll call you when I get home."

Eve collected her coat and walked out of the room. The crisp weather did nothing to calm the sweltering heat pulsing through her veins. What she didn't know was if that resulted from being near Kane again or if it was adrenaline because of the threatening email she received.

2

—————

PRESENT DAY

Eve stared at the contents of her fridge. She knew what choice she should make versus the choice she was likely to make. With a huff, she closed the door, grabbed a cup, and filled it with water. Counting that as her win for the day, she walked into her living room and grabbed the remote she had tossed on her couch the night before. She turned on the television, changed it to her favorite morning news show, and listened as she finished getting ready for the day.

About an hour and a half later, Eve dashed into the *Capitol Express* offices. She had wanted to arrive at the office earlier but had woken up late. Thankfully, she was already ahead on a deadline she had to meet for the day, so she wasn't too far behind.

Eve worked for the *Capitol Express* as their congressional affairs reporter. One of her more recent projects was to interview the incoming class of congressional freshmen, which would then be published on the *Capitol Express*'s website. It was to give the public an opportunity to meet the newly elected. She wasn't the only journalist working on this project, but it was still time consuming. Not that she minded. Eve preferred to keep busy, sometimes to her own detriment. Sometimes she volunteered for or was told to complete too many projects, leading her to become overwhelmed and exhausted.

She reached her cubicle and placed her vending machine Coke on her desk. The smell of coffee hung in the air, but Eve preferred the cold tingle that came with drinking soda. One quick look at the clock told her that it was almost time for the newsroom meeting. She grabbed her book bag one more and threw it over one shoulder before grabbing her laptop and heading into one of the bigger conference rooms on her floor.

This meeting usually offered an opportunity to assess how everything went since the last meeting, to showcase who has done a phenomenal job recently, and to pitch and discuss new ideas. It was one of the meetings that Eve looked forward to each week because it gave her more of an opportunity to collaborate with her coworkers.

As Eve walked down the hall, she smiled at, Tara, a fellow reporter, who was headed in the opposite direction. She had just come back from maternity leave about a week ago.

"Having a good morning?" Tara asked as the two walked past each other.

"Yep. Are you going to make the meeting?"

Tara looked stunned before realization hit her like a ton of bricks. "It's okay to blame this on mom brain, right?"

Eve chuckled. "I don't know anything about that, but I assume you can. Lack of sleep doesn't help either, I'm sure."

"You're right. Let me put this down at my desk and I'll meet you there."

"I'll save you a seat."

Tara smiled, thanked Eve, and continued on her way while Eve strolled down the hall to the conference room. She took a seat and placed her bag on the seat next to her for Tara. It didn't take long for Tara to make her way through the door and Eve moved her bag.

"Thank you," said Tara.

"Good morning."

Eve and Tara looked over and found their coworker Liam sitting diagonally behind them. The women gave a small smile and waved before Tara whispered, "Is he still at it?"

"What do you mean?" Eve whispered back, not wanting to draw much attention to them.

"Flirting with you any chance he gets."

"I don't know if I would consider it flirting."

Before Tara could respond, someone near the front of the room cleared their throats and the meeting began.

THE MEETING DIDN'T LAST AS LONG as Eve expected and soon she was back at her desk. With her book bag near her feet and her laptop in its charging dock, she got to work. She was finishing up another story she had pitched to her boss a couple of days ago — now due by lunchtime.

A few hours later, Eve leaned back in her office chair and closed her eyes. She sent the story to her boss with minutes to spare. She figured now was time to take a ten-second breather before she dug her teeth into something new.

"Want a cup of coffee?"

Eve jumped in her chair and turned to the voice that had interrupted her.

"Liam. Hey, sorry, I didn't hear you come over here." Eve mentally chastised herself for saying sorry for something she shouldn't be sorry about. It was something she was working on stopping.

In terms of Liam, she had a feeling that he might be interested in her, based on some of their interactions over the course of his time at the *Capitol Express*. He hadn't been inappropriate to her, but her gut told her there might be more than friendly feelings from him. He always volunteered to help when she needed it, and he dropped by her cubicle like this a couple of times a week. She glanced at Liam before turning her attention back to her computer. She checked to see if she'd received any emails and then looked at him once more.

"Can you repeat that?"

Liam repeated his offer and Eve shook her head. "No, thank you, but I appreciate it."

He shrugged in return. "I was on my way to the break room, so I figured I'd ask. Let me know if I can get you anything."

Eve smiled. "Will do. We should probably get everyone together to talk about these congressional interviews."

Liam shifted his feet and nodded his head. "Sounds like a plan. I'll look to see if I can schedule a meeting in the next couple of days." He paused for a moment before he said, "I'll see you around." And he walked away.

Eve shook off the encounter and got to work. She had a list of sources she needed to call to figure out what her next story was going to be.

THE DAY PASSED by in a flash and the next thing Eve knew, she was packing up to leave the office for the night. She had brought a change of clothes with her so she could go to barre class straight from work. Eve waved to some of her coworkers on her way out the door and quickly changed in the office bathroom. When she finished, she took the elevator down to the lobby and darted out the front doors. A quick glance at her watch told her that she had twenty minutes to get to class, giving her about five minutes of prep time before the class began. She got there with about five minutes to spare; thankfully, the studio wasn't too far from her job.

Although Rae and Jules both lived in Virginia now and Liv could come only every so often, Eve continued to go to the barre studio they used to frequent. It gave her an opportunity to do something for herself, especially in a time when it felt as if she was always running from place to place at warp speed.

Her mind drifted back to thoughts of the last happy hour with her best friends and how Rae brought up Kane. In fact, every time someone mentioned his name, or when he walked in the room, memories of the night they spent together crashed into her mind like a runaway train careening into a brick wall. She kept their one-night stand a secret because she didn't want the pressure. She didn't want to do anything about it, and she never thought she would see him again. Then Rae had to run into Flint, tossing Kane back into her life once more.

The barre teacher interrupted her thoughts when she told her students that class was about to begin. She thanked the teacher in her mind because the last thing she needed to be doing was thinking about Kane. Eve spent the rest of the class focusing on her moves versus everything else that was going on in the world.

Her trip back to her apartment was uneventful. Eve threw leftover spaghetti in the microwave to eat before she passed out. While she was waiting for her dinner, she prepared a ham and cheese sandwich.

"Plus, one for me thinking ahead and attempting to save money," she mumbled, placing the sandwich in the fridge, planning to take it with her to work tomorrow. The rest of her evening remained uneventful, but who knew what tomorrow would bring.

3

───────

"Eve, do you have a moment?" Eve's eyes flew off her monitor, and she was shocked to find her boss, Casey, standing in front of her.

"Sure, what do you need?"

"Do you mind running up to the Hill and interviewing Representative Blake again? I know you're working on another project, but Ariel couldn't make—"

"Yep. Sure. Not a problem." Eve knew she sounded too eager, but she didn't care. This was a chance she hadn't expected to fall into her lap. She thanked her lucky stars that Casey had even thought to ask her to take on this last-minute assignment.

"I'll forward the email with the list of questions she wanted to ask."

"Sounds good. When is the interview?"

Casey checked her watch. "In about an hour."

Eve had enough wiggle room to get stuff together and head over to Capitol Hill without being in a full panic. Her cab pulled up to the Rayburn House Office Building with plenty of time to spare. Because she was on the Hill so frequently, she had no issue locating Representative Blake's congressional office. Eve walked into his office, let the intern at the front desk know who she was, and sat down until they called her in to see the congressman.

She took that time to scan the questions Ariel had left for her and to give herself a small pep talk. She needed to remain cool and professional because she would come face-to-face with the person who triggered her investigation into this matter: Kayla Harper.

"Eve, hello." The person in question appeared in front of her. Nothing about her expression told Eve that Kayla knew what Eve overheard. Today, she wore a dark brown dress and black heels. Her auburn hair was pulled into a low bun, and a small pearl necklace finished the outfit.

"Kayla, it's nice to see you again." That was both the truth and a lie, but Eve couldn't determine which outweighed the other at that moment. The two women shook hands and Kayla led Eve into the congressman's office.

"Anthony should be back in a bit, but he didn't want to keep you waiting."

Eve waved her off. "No worries. How's the start of the year treating you?" Eve figured small talk couldn't hurt.

"I mean, outside of the normal craziness that comes with the start of a new year, things are good." Based on the wavering of her voice when she uttered the last words of her sentence, Eve thought she was just being polite versus telling the truth.

"Same for me, but I assume for different reasons."

Kayla chuckled at Eve's statement. "Potentially, but our lives may be more similar than you think."

Her words made Eve look up. Kayla was looking at the awards that the congressman had hung in his office. Were those words directed at her, or was there no second meaning to them? Judging by the look on her face, Eve thought she meant nothing by it.

Before Eve or Kayla could say anything else, Representative Blake breezed into the room. His furrowed brow changed as he shifted his gaze from his phone to the women in his office. "Eve, I'm sorry I'm late. Got held up at my last meeting. Kayla, thanks for getting started without me."

Although the congressman was late, you couldn't tell it by looking at him. He hadn't rushed into the room like a tornado apologizing for his tardiness. His black suit fit him perfectly without a wrinkle in sight. Not a strand of his blond hair was out of place. Anyone could sense the confidence in his aura as well as see it in his bright green eyes. He was several inches taller than her; Eve was pretty sure the congressman could be a model if he wanted to be.

Kayla nodded her head in acknowledgment but said nothing. Representative Blake gestured for the women to sit at the table in the corner of his office. He turned his attention to Eve and said, "Shall we get started?"

Eve agreed and took out her recorder and phone. She always had both devices with her when interviewing someone on the record. With the increasing need to fact-check interviewees, Eve made it a point to hand over her recordings to professionals whose job it was to make sure recorded statements were accurate. She also kept a notebook on hand to jot down notes or to use as a prop, depending on what the situation called for.

Throughout her experience with interviewing, Eve found that having a notebook out and writing notes often jogged her memory later when she was drafting an article. Plus, someone's body language could tell how they really felt or what they meant more than their words could.

"First, I wanted to thank you both for having me here. This interview should be relatively quick. I know you both have busy schedules." Eve usually said this before her interviews because she wanted the person she was interviewing to know that she thought their time was valuable. She felt that this would start the interview off on the right foot.

Eve focused most of the questions on the congressman's record and on his goals for the new term. Near the end of interview, Eve shifted gears and asked about a few more personal matters.

Eve glanced down at her notepad before looking up at the congressman.

"You got married just before the election last year. How's married life treating you?"

A smile crept onto his face. "So far? It's been great. We had a decent-sized wedding, so it wasn't hard to plan. Wait, don't let Isabel know I said that. I admit she did most of the prep work in planning for it because of the election. So, I guess I shouldn't say that it was smooth sailing because I wasn't involved in most of it. But we had a great time and are settling into newlywed life."

"And it took place in your hometown, correct?"

"Yes. My hometown is about two hours away from here, so our friends in D.C. could make the drive. It was great to see family and old friends in the week leading up to and at the wedding."

"And is it true that your father officiated the ceremony?"

"Yes, he did. He's the mayor of my hometown, which made it easy to set up and pick a date, and that I can comment on because my wife involved me in it."

All parties chuckled at the congressman's admission. Eve made a small note to herself that only she could decipher to do some more research into the Blake family. His father was involved in politics too? It would be an interesting development and might provide another element to the story.

Eve asked a couple more questions before concluding the interview. "Well, that's that."

"Perfect. Once again, I apologize for being late, and we can't wait to see the article."

Eve nodded her head. "It was not a problem. I'm sure I'll be in close contact with Kayla as we move to produce the finished piece."

Representative Blake held out his hand and Eve gave him a firm handshake before turning to Kayla. The two shook hands as well, and Eve waved at the intern on her way out the door.

Once Eve was seated in the back of a cab, on her way back to her office, she pulled out the notebook that she used during her interview with Congressman Blake. Skimming her notes, she came across Mayor Blake's name. His name was followed by an R with a circle around it. She pulled out her phone and quickly typed in his name. It didn't take long for the results to appear on the screen and she scanned them quickly.

"Jeff Blake." She mumbled to herself. "Married for over

forty years, has lived in Capitol his whole life..." She continued reading but found nothing extraordinary. He had been the town's mayor for over twenty-five years and showed no signs of retiring anytime soon. Eve lowered the volume of her phone and tapped a video. She listened to a couple of minutes of a speech that Mayor Blake had given in front of his constituents. She then muted the video but continued to watch. "I can see where Congressman Blake got his charisma and knack for politics from."

"Miss?"

Eve looked up at the cab driver before looking out of the window closest to her. "Oh, we are here!" She threw every-thing but her phone into her bag and confirmed that the payment for her trip was made. "Thanks so much."

"Not a problem, Miss."

Eve scrambled to get out of the car and briefly looked back, making sure she grabbed all of her belongings. She did. She closed the door and headed into her office building.

A FEW HOURS LATER, Eve had just finished up a sentence when her phone rang.

"The *Capitol Express*, Eve Jackson speaking."

"It's Hugo. I might have some information on a certain congressman."

Eve sat up straight in her chair. "Where do you want to meet?"

"Our usual. In twenty minutes if that works for you?"

"See you then." Eve repacked her bag and left her office in record time.

EVE'S fast pace left her breathless, but she made it with two minutes to spare. She walked into the Hive, a hole-in-the-wall bar not too far from her office. The bar had been around for over forty years and, much like the Green Hat, reminded Eve of quintessential D.C. It wasn't designed as nicely as her favorite happy hour spot. The lighting in the bar could be brighter; it wasn't quite 4:00, but that didn't stop the bar from setting the mood for the patrons that left work early for drinks on the menu. It took some maneuvering for Eve to make her way toward the back of the bar where she usually met Hugo. Hugo was already there waiting for her.

His long, waist-length blond hair looked as if it hadn't been washed in about two weeks. His clothes didn't look much better based on what she could see. But, according to him, this look was in and it was what he preferred. He spoke before she uttered a word.

"Glad you could make it."

"You didn't give me much choice, nor a lot of warning."

Hugo moved his head from side to side, as if he were thinking about the comment. "I figured you would want this information right off the presses." He paused for a moment and snorted at his pun. "After all, I'm not sure how long it will be before other members of the press get wind of this."

"Well, get to it. I don't have all night."

"And all of this stays off the record, correct?"

"Yes. Everything said here will be off the record."

He leaned forward, hands clasped in front of him on the table, and gave Eve a smirk. "You know how you called me about Congress's golden boy?"

"Yes." What a coincidence that Hugo's information about Representative Blake would come on the same day she just happened to interview him.

"Now, I don't know the specific details, but your hunch was right. The squeaky-clean image that he portrays in public is just that. A manufactured image. Apparently, he has a bit of a past, but I don't know much more than that. They sealed a lot of what he got into."

"Look, if he did some things when he was a kid and it was scrubbed from his record—"

"If by kid you mean in his twenties then sure."

The interruption made Eve pause. "Early twenties? Mid-twenties? Can you give me anything else to go on?"

"I would say early twenties and it's bad enough that you might have a hard time finding out information about it, even in the age of the internet."

Eve huffed. "Why can't you be straightforward about things like this?"

"Because I have to keep my sources private, just like you have to do in your line of work."

At least they could agree on that. "So, it looks like I need to do some digging." She said that more to herself than to the man in front of her.

"I'd say. Sometimes people want things to stay buried, but, as the saying goes, what's done in the dark will come out in the light. Well, I think that's how it goes."

"It sounds good to me. Do you have anything else?"

Hugo shook his head. "But I have your number if I hear anything."

Eve stood up, grabbed her bag, and left the establishment.

What she didn't know was that someone was watching her every move, hoping for an opportunity to put an end to her investigation.

4

———

"Think she'll ever get here?"

Eve spared a glance at Liv before she shrugged. She knew the drill by now. Rae couldn't get to their happy hours on time to save her life.

"And here you go, ladies." Eve looked up and saw John to her left. He gave each woman a small smile as he placed their drink orders in front of them. He also placed a glass of water in front of the empty place at the table. "Anything else I can get you?"

"Rough day today?" Eve looked over at Jules to see what she was talking about. She followed Jules's gaze and a small gasp left her lips. Liv had ordered a rum and Coke and a shot of tequila. Liv had volunteered to walk up to the bar and order their drinks but hadn't shared what she was ordering before she left. And now Eve knew why.

"Work continues to get more and more complicated." Eve watched as Liv didn't wait for a response from her friends before taking the shot. She shook her head and closed her eyes tight before she popped them open and said, "WHOA."

"I'm sure that burned on the way down."

"It did. Just a bit."

Eve shook her head before a shiver coursed through her body. She looked toward the front door of the Green Hat because she assumed that someone had entered the establishment and thought it might have been Rae. But she was wrong. There was still no sign of Rae, the fourth friend in their crew.

"Has Rae contacted either of you?" Jules must have read her mind because as she said those words, Eve was reaching for her phone, which was still in her book bag at her feet. A quick tap on the screen confirmed that she had no messages from Rae.

"No," Eve and Liv said at the same time; they looked at each other. Liv burst out laughing and Eve could see Jules doing everything she could to hold it together. Jules lasted about a second more before she burst out laughing. Eve soon joined in and the three women had tears streaming down their faces.

"What did I miss?"

Eve looked up and found her missing friend. Rae tossed a long, dark brown curl over her shoulder as she sat at the table. The other women sobered up and wiped the tears from their eyes.

"About time you showed up. Everything okay?" Liv asked.

"Everything is fine. Still busy, but fine."

"Cheers to that," mumbled Eve before she sloshed her drink around in her glass.

"How is everything going with your 'get to know your Members of Congress' project?"

"It's going okay. A lot of work, but that was to be expected given that Congress will be back in session soon. I had something weird happen to me a couple of months ago though. I might have on the scoop on another story."

Eve watched as the other women leaned closer to hear what she was going to say. "Rae, don't you want to order something first?"

"You can't leave us hanging like that!" Eve gave a sideways glance to Liv after her dramatic exclamation.

"My drink can wait. What did you find out?"

Eve retold the events that occurred after her interview. The other ladies hung on to her every word until she finished telling the story.

"So, it could be nothing, but it could be something huge?"

Eve rolled Jules's comment around in her head for a moment before nodding. "That sounds about right. But I can't get the conversation out of my mind. I've called a few of the people I've worked on scoops with before, but either they hadn't heard of it or they haven't gotten back to me yet. So, right now, I research and wait."

"Be careful, okay? After all the craziness of the last year, I think we all deserve some peace and quiet." Eve knew that Rae was referring to the drama that had surrounded her and her fiancé, Flint West. Eve was happy that they persevered through the chaos that surrounded them. Now Flint was a part of the incoming class of congressional members, and they were in the beginning stages of picking a wedding date. "You know if you're investigating what this might be, maybe it's worth bringing up to Kane—"

"Rae, you already know how I feel about Kane. I asked him for help to get me into the veterans' event that helped us trap Cassandra. That's it on that front."

Rae held her hands up. "Okay, okay. I was just trying to help and think of a potential way for you to gain more information. That's it."

Eve's gaze floated from Rae to Liv to Jules. She could see that at least one of them knew that this wasn't only about trying to gain more information. Eve sighed and said, "If I'm desperate I'll contact him, okay? He already has somewhat of an idea of what's going on based on what happened at your engagement party."

"Wait a minute. Did we miss what happened at the party? Liv, did you know?" Jules's eyes jumped from her to Liv and back again, searching for an answer to the problem at hand.

Liv shook her head. "No. I had no idea. Rae, is any of this recent information for you?"

Rae took a deep breath. "I knew a bit about what was going on because Eve got a threatening message while at the engagement party. Kane was nearby when all this went down."

Eve could feel the change in the room as Jules and Liv came to terms with the current state of affairs. "Listen, I kept most of this to myself because this isn't unfamiliar territory for me. Although it isn't common, you know I've been threatened on the job before." The looks that passed between the friends ranged between sympathy and sadness. "I didn't want anyone to worry because usually the threats die down eventually. It's a part of the risk of doing my job. My boss knows and the proper authorities have been notified, but there isn't much we can do because the person hasn't physically harmed me."

"You mentioned something like this happened before.

Does this time feel different?" Jules's voice was just above a whisper.

"I think so."

SEVERAL DAYS LATER, Eve sat in her cubicle working on a project she needed to complete. It was well past quitting time, but Eve had stayed to get the project done. Out of the corner of her eye, Eve saw something and swung her head around, nearly causing her headphones to fly out of her ears. Her heart rate slowed a bit when she noticed that it was Liam standing at the entrance of her cubicle.

"On a deadline?" he asked after she removed the earbuds from her ears.

"When am I not?" she said, stretching her arms behind her.

"Good point," Liam said as he shifted on his feet and adjusted his coat. "You know I was wondering if maybe you wanted to go out for a drink sometime?"

"Do you mean as a date?"

Liam nodded but said nothing.

"Liam, you're a great guy, but I'm not comfortable dating someone I work with. You know, just in case something goes wrong, I don't want it to carry over into my work life." It wasn't a lie. Having something spill over into the workplace would be a disaster.

Liam nodded and said, "I understand. That makes sense. Well, I'm going to head out now. You should probably go home, too, since it's late."

Eve looked down at the clock on her laptop and noticed

that he was right. It was well after 7:00 and she was still in the office. Not that that was unheard of, depending on what story she was working. She then stood up and looked around the office and noticed that no one else was around either.

"Damn, I didn't realize how late it was." She stretched again. "I'm going to finish up what I'm doing and then leave. Thanks for the heads-up."

"Don't mention it. I'll see you around." With that, Liam left, and she sat down to continue her work once more. Her fingers flew over the keyboard as she put the finishing touches on a smaller article about the current political landscape.

"Excuse me, Eve."

Eve looked up and saw that the cleaning crew was making their way around the office to spruce up the office before everyone returned to their desks the next day. One woman, Gemma, usually helped clean Eve's floor and since Eve stayed late more nights than she'd like to admit, she and Gemma exchanged pleasantries. Once Gemma was on her way, Eve went back to finishing up the article.

By the time she was finished and doing exercises to stretch out her fingers and hands, it was 8:00. She twisted her neck back and forth, trying to work out the kinks as she read over her work, deciding if there was anything she wanted to add before calling it a night. Halfway into her read-through, the main lights in the office cut off.

"Huh," mumbled Eve. She looked around to see what the heck was going on. Gemma usually kept the lights on for her and Eve would turn them off as she left. Thankfully, it wasn't dark enough that Eve couldn't see anything, so she closed her laptop and put it in her book bag in one swift motion. She fumbled around for a second before grabbing her charger, phone, and keys. It was probably the best course of action to keep her phone and keys on her just in case she needed them.

As she was about to stand up, goosebumps traveled over her body and the hairs on her arm stood on edge. Something about this felt very wrong. Cementing that feeling was the slam of a door across the office suite, and she all but jumped out of her chair. *I might be paranoid, but I'm not about to find out if I'm wrong.*

With the book bag on her back, Eve sprinted across two rows of cubicles, mentally thanking her long legs for taking her across the next row of cubicles in record time. She peeked around the last row but saw no one. Her heart pounded in her ears, so much she almost couldn't hear herself think. She sprinted toward the exit.

Eve debated whether to take the elevator or the stairs when the elevator doors opened in front of her. She quickly hopped on and pressed the close door button. As the doors were about to close, a brown bag flew in between them, stopping their movement. Eve's eyes fixated on the bag as the doors reopened, revealing a petite young woman who smiled at Eve before stepping into the elevator.

"Sorry about that. My feet were hurting from wearing these shoes all day and I didn't want to wait for the next elevator."

Eve looked down at the woman's feet and the heels in her hand and sucked in a deep breath to calm her racing heart. Her mind was playing tricks on her. She couldn't place her; had they met before? Maybe she worked on another floor in their building. She definitely wasn't someone she saw on a regular basis. Eve nodded her head in acknowledgment, but she didn't trust her voice not to quiver — although she wanted to ask her more questions. She shouldn't have dug into this case.

But there was no way she could let it go now.

5

———

Later the next day, Eve was wrapping up a phone call when the woman from the elevator appeared in her cubicle.

"Hi, you're Eve Jackson, right? I'm Lily. We met last night in the elevator."

Eve's eyes darted from left to right before landing on the woman in front of her. "Yes? How can I help you?"

"This was left for you at the front desk." Lily held out a manila envelope.

Eve wasn't expecting a delivery of any kind, let alone at her office. "Did you notice anything about the person who delivered it? Anything that was unusual?"

"Nope. He was our regular delivery guy. Is something wrong?"

Eve shook her head, not wanting to draw more attention to the situation in case she was overreacting. But her gut told her she wasn't.

"Thanks for bringing this to me."

"Don't mention it. See you around!" Lily gave Eve a small wave before leaving her alone.

The first thing Eve looked for was a return address. Seeing none made her even more wary about the contents of the letter. Figuring that, at this point, curiosity was going to get the best of her and she had nothing to lose, she opened the envelope and found a letter.

Eve,

We know you overheard something you shouldn't have in the U.S. Capitol. We know you've continued digging into a situation that doesn't involve you. Drop your investigation or else.

The letter was unsigned.

The piece of paper dropped from her hands and landed on the floor like a feather falling from a pillow. Eve could feel herself shaking as the words raced through her mind. Figuring she it wouldn't be wise to cause a scene, she scrambled to pick up the letter and crammed it into her book bag. Sending a quick message to her boss about suddenly not feeling well, Eve packed up the rest of her things and darted out of her office. She needed to get home now.

After a few tries, Eve inserted her front door key into the lock. With a decisive snap, the door opened and Eve rushed into her apartment. Before she could stop it, she lost control of the door and it slammed shut. *Bang.* The loud noise was the last thing her nerves needed. She took a deep breath as she tried to calm her racing heart. At least she was home. She shoved her hands into her short, dark brown strands, trying to relieve some tension that had made its way to her head.

"Eve, calm down and think about this clearly." Her pep talk did little to help shake the feeling running through her veins. She hurried over to her window. Eve slid her finger in between the blinds and gently bent one down, hoping to not attract any attention in case someone was watching her home. Seeing nothing but the remnants of a beautiful sunset, she backed away from the window and breathed a sigh of relief. Her hands made their way through her pixie cut once more before she threw herself on the couch, jacket and shoes and all.

The ringing of her phone startled her. Eve pulled the phone out of her pocket and saw that Rae was trying to reach her.

"Hello?"

"You sound out of breath. Are you okay?"

"Yeah, everything is fine. Why wouldn't it be?"

"You've seemed distant lately."

Eve closed her eyes, taking another second to calm down. Rae already had enough pressure on her, given everything that was going on with her and Flint. Eve didn't want to add to that stress.

"I think we've both been busy. Between you getting engaged, then going on vacation, and now Flint getting sworn in next week it's been difficult to chat. Not to mention the holidays and my own work deadlines thrown into the mix. But no, I swear everything is fine." The mostly accurate statements sounded fantastic, even to her own ears.

"Are you sure nothing else is up?"

"Nope," Eve said, the lie falling from her lips with ease. She would've felt bad about not telling Rae everything — but Rae had had enough things to deal with due to outside forces trying to destroy her relationship. Eve figured the best thing was to deal with her situation alone.

"Are you still able to make it to the minor celebration we

are having in Flint's new office after his swearing-in ceremony?"

Eve nodded her head, although Rae couldn't see her, and then said, "I wouldn't miss it for anything." Flint's staff were throwing together a small meet-and-greet type of event at his office.

Bang.

The noise almost forced Eve off of her couch. The sound that fell from her lips did nothing to help reassure Rae that something wasn't going on with her friend.

"Are you sure that everything is all right?"

"Yeah. That noise was because my upstairs neighbor is lifting weights and sometimes likes to slam them down on the floor. You would think by now that I'd be used to it." Eve paused and stood up from her lounging position on the couch. "And before you say that this isn't something I should have to get used to... I know. Yes, I've complained about it, but nothing has changed because I'm still dealing with it. Yes, I'm also looking at other apartments."

She headed into her small but functional kitchen and pulled out a cold soda. She cracked it open and was happy to let the fizzy drink flow down her throat. Everyone kept telling her that her habit of drinking one to two cans of soda a day would catch up with her, but so far it hadn't.

"Did you hear anything else from whoever left that email for you?"

Eve choked on her drink and coughed to clear her throat. "Sorry. I was drinking when you said that." Eve grabbed a paper towel and wiped her mouth. "No, I have heard nothing from whoever sent me that email some time ago. I assume it was someone playing a prank." That's a lie.

"Are you sure? I could ask Kane to—"

"No. That is perfectly okay. Like I said, it's just a prank." Still a lie.

"We take pranks seriously now. I think even if it's nothing, Kane would have no problem looking into this for you."

"Rae, everything is fine. But if anything changes, I'll let you know." *Debatable. But I know I won't be telling Kane anything else. And that is because I don't trust him.*

"Okay. I'm always here for you. And I truly appreciate everything you did to help."

Eve's head snapped back, and she looked down at her phone. She knew Rae felt that way but hadn't expected her to say it. It made her uncomfortable in a way because she felt that what she had done was an automatic response to her friend being in danger. "No worries. I did what any sensible person would have done."

Rae cleared her throat before she responded. "Anyway, I wanted to check in, but I'll let you go."

"Thanks, girl. I'll talk to you later." Eve's lips twitched into a smile. "Bye." She ended the call and another bang from upstairs made her jump.

"Asshole," she mumbled as she headed toward her bedroom. The somewhat cramped one-bedroom apartment in Washington, D.C., had been her home for the last three years. Although she debated moving to have more room, the time and effort required to take on that monumental task was the last thing on her mind. She walked over to the desk in the corner of her bedroom; it was covered in pieces of most, if not all, of the articles she had worked on recently.

"I really need to clean this up," she said as she leaned down to pick up some papers that had fallen off her desk. Eve set the papers in a neat pile in the corner of her desk and as a result knocked over a cup of pens and markers. She sighed as she bent over to pick them up. Once the writing utensils were back in their proper place, she turned around and examined the corkboard on the wall next to her desk. Sketches, notes, and other research about Representative Anthony Blake took over most of the space on the board.

She hadn't realized how much what she overheard a few months before had taken over her life. Figuring she had nothing else to do, she opened her laptop and started researching Representative Blake once more. Details related to bills he cosponsored, events he attended, quotes in the news, et cetera. She wouldn't stop until she found out what the congressman was hiding.

6

———

Eve stood in the corner of Flint's congressional office and watched the scene before her. A familiar voice interrupted her thoughts.

"Eve, this is not okay." Eve adjusted her body and cast a look at Jules. She did her best to mask her feelings, but figured it was pointless because of how well she and Jules knew each other.

"I have a handle on it."

"Do you? Because all of this seems to be escalating versus calming down." Eve could probably count on one hand how many times Jules has snapped on anyone in their friend group. It took a lot to get her to that point. Jules took a deep breath before she continued. "I'm worried about you. That's all."

"Everything is—"

"Fine?" Rae would choose this opportunity to leave Flint's side and appear next to them. "Is someone still trying to get you to stop investigating what you overheard Kayla Harper talking about?"

"Can you speak a little louder? I'm sure the Speaker of the House didn't hear you."

"I already told you, at the very least, you should talk to Kane about all of this."

"Talk to me about what?"

Eve closed her eyes and tried to practice some breathing techniques she learned online. Nothing could go her way today, could it?

"Eve is still getting threatening messages. You know, like the one I mentioned to you after she left my engagement party?"

"Do you want me to look into anything?" At least he had the decency to lower his voice to not attract attention. After all, this congressional office wasn't that big to begin with.

Eve sighed before she shrugged. "Can we talk about it after the festivities here end?" Once she explained everything to him, she figured he would see things her way and she would get everyone off her back. He nodded before walking over to Flint. Her brave mask fell slightly when she felt his eyes on her from across the room.

EVE GLANCED up and then back down at her phone as she checked her messages on her way out of Longworth House Office Building. She walked right out onto Independence Avenue and debated whether she wanted to catch a cab here or walk across the Capitol to Union Station where she could take the Metro home. She hesitated briefly before stepping out of her heels and putting her flats on. Maybe the crisp air and a pleasant walk would help clear her mind.

She waited for the walk sign to turn a steady white before she started crossing the busy street. She was halfway across when she heard her name. Eve turned around briefly, looked behind her and almost stopped in the middle of the street. There stood Kane, looking at her from across the road. When she turned back around to continue crossing, the piercing noise of a car horn blaring startled her, causing her to stumble over her own feet. Eve looked at the car whose driver had slammed his hand down on the horn and back up at the walk sign, noting that she still had the right of way.

"What the—" She wasn't sure what had caused Kane to stop midsentence, but a sense of relief washed over her when she felt his hand on the small of her back; he led her across the street just before the walk signal turned to red. "Are you okay?"

"I—I think so?" If she hadn't been freaked out by almost seeing her life flash before her eyes, she would have rolled her eyes at herself. She moved away from him, and his hand drifted from her and back to his side. His eyes scanned her face, probably trying to detect if she was really hurt. "I'm fine and thanks. That was a little crazy, however." She gestured to the street behind them.

"I agree. Are you sure you're okay?"

Eve nodded before she took a deep breath. A fake smile followed that deep breath. "I'm good. I'm going to head home and hopefully not almost get hit by any more cars."

"Wait, didn't you want to talk about the case you're looking into?"

Why had she thought he might have forgotten about that? His question hung in the air and Eve got a whiff of his cologne. It was subtle enough that she almost thought she dreamed it, but she smelled another trace of the aroma and confirmed that she wasn't mistaken. The light fragrance was mixed with a hint of woodsy edge, which was how Eve would describe Kane. Memories from the night they spent together flooded her brain as she thought about that smell on his sheets, that smell on him, that smell on her.

"You will not let this go, huh?"

"Nope. I know we rarely see eye to eye, but—"

"Kane, you know exactly why we aren't friendly, even though we've been forced to be around each other over the last year. I appreciate that you got me into the veterans' event that eventually led to us catching Cassandra and Rob, but that's where anything related to us begins and ends."

"That's not how it always was."

It took a lot to keep Eve from stopping in her tracks and glaring at Kane. But the crisp wind on her face and a desire to get home as soon as possible stopped her. "Kane." She paused and glanced at him out of the corner of her eye. "It was one night years ago. Emphasis on years."

"One night that we both won't ever forget."

That comment brought Eve to a halt. "I thought we said we wouldn't ever talk about that night."

"That was your idea. I followed along with it, because that's what you wanted, but at some point, we are going to talk about it."

Eve shrugged before she said, "I thought we were supposed to be talking about a more pressing matter?" She hoped her words showed how indifferent she was to him and his desire to talk about the night they slept together. Well, there had been little sleeping involved.

"You're right. What's going on with you getting threatened? Is this anything like what happened to Rae and Flint?"

Eve shook her head. "Honestly, I'd rather it be something similar to that versus what's happening to me. I overheard a staffer from a congressman's office talking about a secret that must be kept buried. Well, that wouldn't remain true around a journalist, right? If it's a story that his constituents and the public need to know, it's my job to shine a light on it. Well, someone doesn't want me to, and they have been making their point loud and clear. Granted it's only been through messages, but I assume it might escalate."

Kane didn't answer right away. Eve took the time to look at the U.S. Capitol as they walked past one of the most majestic buildings in Washington, D.C. She had almost forgotten she asked him a question until he finally replied.

"Interesting. Sounds mysterious but dangerous and totally something that would happen in D.C."

"What do you mean?"

"Ah, nothing. Thinking something like this wouldn't be as likely to happen where I'm from."

"Famous last words. I thought you grew up in the area, too."

"Nope, but I wasn't too far. About a two-hour drive from here."

"I didn't know that." Eve waited a beat before she continued. "I started looking into what might be the secret. Researching, asking a couple of people questions here and there. I thought I was doing so quietly, but, apparently, I'm not. I assume I'm getting too close for comfort because I received an email to my work account about laying off the case. That was the email I got the night of Flint and Rae's engagement party." The wind picked up, causing a piece of hair to fly into her face. She swept the hair back into place before putting her hand in her coat pocket. "Then I got another letter in the mail recently at my job."

"Are the police involved?"

Eve nodded. "Somewhat. They know about the email, but I haven't told them about the letter yet. There isn't much they can do because whoever is sending them has done nothing criminal yet. But at least it's on their radar? I don't know."

"Have you noticed any other strange occurrences?"

Eve thought back to the incident at her office that made her wonder if she was being paranoid or not and figured that was something worth mentioning. "I don't know if I was just exhausted or what, but I thought someone was playing tricks on me the other day."

Kane motioned for her to keep going, so she did. "I was in the office late one night and I swore someone was trying to freak me out. Someone turned the lights out while I was still at my desk."

"Could it have been a mistake?"

"Of course, which is why I debated telling you. There have been smaller incidents here and there, but I could always write them off as my imagination or a coincidence."

"I don't believe in coincidences."

Neither do I. At least we can agree on that. "I'm glad we agree about that."

She mentally hit herself because she hadn't realized she said the words out loud. Kane's smirk in her direction almost sent her into another fit of memories, including ones where he sent that smirk after he—

"Do you mind if I go home with you?"

His question did nothing to remove the memories of that night and raised her guard. "Why?"

"Because I have a feeling that a lot of these incidents aren't you reading too much into something. I'll look around your place with you to see if we find anything."

Eve debated with herself for a moment before she dipped her head. Although she wasn't particularly thrilled with having Kane in her home, she figured there was no harm in it. "Sure, let's go."

"DOES your apartment have a garage where you can park your car?"

"We have outdoor parking. In fact, my car is just up the road. The burgundy sedan," she said. Eve pointed her car out for Kane and when she turned toward her apartment, he kept walking.

"I'll check this out first."

Eve stared at his back for a moment before following. He walked around the car twice and bent down to look underneath. She heard him mutter something that sounded like a cussword; he shifted his body to the point where he was on one knee and looked up at her. If someone walked by, they might think he was preparing to propose to her. It didn't help that he reached into his back pocket of his slacks.

Eve's eyes widened as she looked at him and back at her car. He pulled out his cell phone with a small smile on his face. And that's when she knew he knew what he was doing.

"I think I see something under your car but wanted to take a photo with my phone for a better look."

"Right."

He bent down again and took several photos before rising to his feet. Kane fiddled around with his phone before turning the screen to Eve to show her the photos. "See that?"

"I do, but I have no idea what that is," she said. She turned the phone from side to side, trying to figure out what the object was, but was still confused. "I assume it's not supposed to be underneath my car?"

Kane confirmed with a shake of his head. "That's a GPS tracker. Someone has been keeping track of you."

Eve rubbed her hands over her face. She had decided to take a breather in her bathroom. Sitting on the edge of her bathtub, she attempted to understand how she was feeling, away from Kane's questioning eyes.

"What the hell am I doing?" She mumbled out loud. Life for her had been reasonably quiet before this potential story had torpedoed into her life. Yet she knew she needed to remain undeterred. She had made a promise to herself to get to the bottom of a story, especially if it needed to be a matter of public record, and that was what she was going to do. Her gut told her that she needed to get to the bottom of this, even though she would be lying to herself if she said she wasn't worried.

Eve stood up, stretching her slim body before turning toward the sink and turning on the spout. It took no time for her to wash her hands, letting the warm water glide over her hands, long after the soap suds faded away. She grabbed one of the hand towels and dried her hands before opening the bathroom door, giving what felt like the rest of the world an opportunity to puncture the armor that she had rebuilt around her emotions.

"Would you like anything to drink? Beer? Soda? Water?" She walked out of the bathroom and headed over to the fridge. Kane sat on her couch, swiping through his smartphone when she marched into the room.

"Could you have any more soda in there?" Eve turned glared at Kane. He gave a pointed look toward the fridge, then focused back on her with a smirk on his face.

"You know it's rude to insult someone who is hosting you, right?"

"Probably, since you could poison my drink. I'll take a water, thanks."

Eve couldn't stop the look that appeared on her face. Apparently, the look was comical to Kane, because he burst out laughing. Now that she thought about it, this might have been the first time she had seen him laugh wholeheartedly. His cheerfulness led a smile to appear on her face, surprising her. With everything going on, he still could make her smile and ease some of the awkwardness that she knew existed between them.

It was weird to have him in her home. It felt intimate in a way that she wasn't expecting. It wasn't like she didn't entertain other people in her private sanctuary, but with him she felt more exposed. She was sure being around him was muddling her thoughts. Or at least that is what she was going to blame it on each time her mind drifted back to the night they spent together and how she wouldn't mind doing that all over again. How had she gotten to this point again?

"Are you okay?"

"Hmm?"

"All of this," Kane gestured to the device on her coffee table. "Is a lot. Are you okay?"

"Yes." The lie fell from her lips with an ease that she wasn't expecting. "Well, do you want to look around?"

"Sure, if you don't mind." Eve was relieved that he dropped the topic.

"Not at all." Eve shrugged and walked over to her couch. She sat there for about a minute before she jumped up and out of her seat. "Shit!"

Kane, who had been checking to see if it looked as if someone had tried to enter the front door, turned around and looked at her. "What's wrong?"

"My bedroom. It's where I keep all of my notes. I'm going to head in there and make sure that nothing was disturbed." Over the last few moments, her emotions were changing on a dime, not boding well for her mental health.

"Sounds good. Holler if you need me."

With that, Eve jogged into her bedroom and made a beeline for her desk. She quickly checked that her documents and corkboard were untouched before she heard the wooden panels creak under what she assumed to be Kane's weight. It wasn't until he cleared his throat that he got her attention. She swung around and found Kane leaning on her doorjamb. "It didn't look like anyone tried to come in through the front door or through any of the windows in your living room. Mind if I look at these windows in here?"

All Eve could do was nod as she watched him stroll into her room and toward the windows. He examined them for a second before he asked, "Did anything looked disturbed on your desk?"

"Nope. I don't think anyone was in here."

"I don't either. It sounds to me for at least right now, whoever this is didn't think it was worth getting into here. But yet they thought it was worth their time to track your movements, specifically if you had to drive somewhere."

"Which is strange because I don't really drive my car. Metro makes things easily accessible."

"Interesting. I don't have many answers, but I could take this device and see if I can find out anything else about it."

Eve had a feeling that it would come to this. She had heard about the secret things that he was into, so maybe he had more resources than she did? She led him out of her bedroom into the living room where the two sat down on her couch. She made sure that he sat down first, so she knew how far to sit away from him. Just because he was helping her, didn't mean she had to like him or enjoy it. She knew she needed to keep this strictly professional.

"Thanks for offering to help. I appreciate it."

Kane leaned forward and downed the glass of water that he had placed on the coffee table earlier. "You have my number in case anything comes up, right?"

Eve thought back to the moment when she was forced to use that number to help Rae trap Cassandra and nodded her head. "Yes, I have it."

With that, he stood up and walked over to her kitchen.

"Don't worry about it. I can take the cup to the sink."

He smirked at her before handing over the cup. Although their fingertips touched only briefly, Eve felt a wave of electricity shoot from her fingertips through her entire body. The only other time she remembered feeling such an electric spark was during their one-night stand years ago. She kept her sigh to herself as she wondered if he felt it too. He gave her an answer when she noticed that he stared at her fingertips, and then her face.

"Let me know if you hear anything and I'll do the same. Be careful." Kane's parting words hung around Eve long after he left her apartment.

7
———

"You know what you're digging into could get you into some scorching water, right?"

"Casey, I know, but I know there's something there and I'm going to find out what it is."

Casey tapped her pen on her lips, clearly thinking about how to approach this situation. Eve briefed her on the latest information she discovered about Congressman Blake.

"Plenty of other reporters have either been stonewalled or have left this case in the dust."

"I know. But I'm not like other reporters."

"I know you aren't. I'm not telling you not to take this case on but know that your other work comes first. I can't stop what you do in your free time."

Eve nodded her head. "Thanks, Casey."

"Don't mention it. But don't forget that the Senator O'Neil piece is due by tomorrow."

Eve sighed, knowing that meant she would probably be up most of the night finishing her draft and the first round of edits on the article. She nodded once more before standing up and heading to the door.

"Eve?"

Eve turned around and looked at her boss.

"Be careful. If you uncover something huge here, there might be a lot of eyes pointed in your direction."

Eve swallowed hard before she opened the door and exited her boss's office.

Back at her desk, Eve scanned the files she had compiled on Representative Blake. He represented a district closer to the middle of the Virginia. Recently got married to his long-time girlfriend and had just been reelected. The photos presented the image of a poised man who joined the world of politics after owning his own profitable small business for almost two decades. The more digging she did, the more she came up empty-handed.

"Representative Anthony Blake. Age thirty-eight. Small business owner. From Capitol, Virginia," Eve mumbled to herself as she read through her notes on what information she had on the subject at hand.

What was she missing? Was this all a wild goose chase? No, it couldn't be. Her instincts were telling her that something was here, and she just needed to find the small thread that, once pulled, would cause everything to unravel. She rubbed her temples to relieve the tension building in her skull, but she knew that any relief would be temporary. The reason for the pain was stress, which probably wasn't going away anytime soon.

The letter she received a couple of weeks ago reared its ugly head every time she thought about Representative Blake. But she was determined not to let this deter her from finding out what she was missing. Plus, she hadn't heard from whoever this was in weeks. Out of sight, out of mind, right?

Her phone vibrating on her desk brought her out of the trance the story usually put her in. The name on the screen caused her heart rate to quicken. It was Kane.

Kane: *I know this is last minute, but would you like to get a drink this evening? I'll be finishing up a meeting around 6:00.*

Part of Eve told her to run away as fast as possible in the other direction. The other part of her wanted to know why he wanted to get drinks... and would that lead to another one-night stand?

Is it called a one-night stand if it happens more than once?

Eve shook her head. Way to go ten steps further than necessary. Figuring she didn't have anything to lose, Eve texted him back.

Eve: *Sure. Want to meet me at Bar Ten at 6:15?*

There. She decided on a place was in between her job and her home, thinking it would be easier for her to go home after... whatever this was.

"Drinks. It's just drinks, Eve." She closed her eyes and opened them again, letting the thoughts of Kane leave her mind so she could concentrate on finishing the day out strong.

Several hours later, she waved goodbye to the security guard at the front desk and went on her way to meet Kane for drinks. Thoughts about what why he wanted to meet flew through her head along with what drink she was going to order. After all, she should celebrate making it through Monday unscathed. It was the little things.

When Eve was a block away from Bar Ten, she waited for

the walk sign to change. When it did, she stepped out into the street and a couple of seconds later, a light out of the corner of her eye caught her attention. She saw the car coming, but it wasn't going too fast. She thought it would stop since they had a red light. Next, tires screeched. That was when she knew something was wrong.

She swung her head back toward the car and she saw that the car had, in fact, sped up and charged at her. *This car is trying to hit me.* The flight or fight moment came, and Eve was temporarily frozen in place. Before she could think further, she felt the wind leave her body. But she didn't land on cold asphalt. No, she landed on something hard, yet warm. When she looked down, she found beautiful hazel eyes staring back at her.

"Kane?" Was this real life? Or was it a mirage she was experiencing because she had a concussion? Either of these options could be true, and she would believe it.

"Are you okay? Did you get hurt anywhere?" The voice sounded real.

"I—I think so?" Eve couldn't stop the quivering of her voice. She had come so close to death that there was no way her heart rate was slowing down anytime soon.

His hands slowly moved down her arms and he studied her face, trying to figure out if she was telling the truth.

"If you're able to move we should probably get across the street before any more cars come."

Eve had forgotten that they were lying down in the middle of traffic.

Just as Eve was about to get up, a woman rushed over to them.

"Are you guys okay?" she asked in a rush. She held out a hand, which Eve took, gladly, to pull herself off of Kane. When she was standing, she realized she missed the comfort of his embrace. Eve looked down and saw that Kane helping himself off the road. It clicked that he had taken the brunt of their fall, and she rushed t to help him up.

"Are you okay?" The fact that he was more worried about her than himself spoke volumes in her mind.

Kane dipped his head once. "Might have some soreness in my back tomorrow, but other than that I feel good." Kane turned to the woman who had helped Eve and asked, "Did you see the accident happen?"

The woman nodded. "I was down the street and saw the aftermath and came rushing over to see if I could help." Her eyes darted toward Eve. "That car was gunning for you. The driver had plenty of opportunity to slow down or swerve but didn't."

"Did you notice anything about the car? Did you see the driver?"

The woman bit her lip before she said, "It was a dark-colored car, maybe black or navy blue. I couldn't see the driver from where I was standing. I was also too far away to get a good look at the license plate."

Eve glanced at Kane as he muttered a curse that confirmed her feelings too. *This might be a dead end.*

"Do you want me to call the police?"

Eve thought that was the logical solution, but Kane hesitated. "I think that's a good idea." She looked at Kane. "Then can we go out for a drink or ten?"

Eve's comment forced Kane to look at her. Although he

nodded and agreed with what she said, she could still see some uncertainty in his eyes.

"I THINK the shock is wearing off. I'm feeling some soreness in my neck." Eve rotated her neck, trying to relieve some tension. Kane saved her life by tackling her to the ground. She wanted to tell him how grateful she was, but she didn't know exactly how to say it.

"Yeah, that back soreness that I predicted? It's definitely starting to creep in." He took a sip of the beer he ordered before setting it back down on the table.

The couple eventually made it to Bar Ten after they spoke to the police; they gave their statements and confirmed that they did not need to be transported to the hospital. After that adventure, Eve planned on enjoying a couple of drinks before going home to take a nice hot shower.

"Thank you."

Kane looked at her with an eyebrow raised. "Thank you for what?"

"For saving my life back there." Eve ran a finger across her glass, not sure what to say to avoid getting emotional. "There's a good chance I would not be here if it weren't for you."

Kane looked down at his beer again before looking directly into her dark brown eyes. "I was waiting for you in front of the bar and noticed you were crossing the street. Then I heard a car revving up its engine. That's when I knew I had to do something because I had a feeling that's what the driver was planning on doing." He leaned forward and grabbed his glass of beer. The look in his eyes showed concern and seriousness. "What is going on?" His voice was barely a whisper.

Eve was uncomfortable with this line of questioning. "I don't you know what you're talking about." She mentally rolled her eyes at herself. What a ridiculous thing to say.

"Eve, you know exactly what I'm talking about. Why would someone want to hurt or kill you?"

"Because I am on the right track to find out something that someone—or people—wants to keep hidden."

Eve's words trailed off as she placed one hand on her neck to provide some relief; her eyes drifted to look at the flat screen TV in one corner of the bar. A warm hand softly landed on hers and that sense of comfort returned. Her eyes flew down to their hands before dancing up to land on his eyes. The heat emitting from his stare brought of memories of their night together and she realized she didn't know one thing.

"Why did you want to go out for drinks?"

Eve couldn't tear her eyes away from Kane even if she tried. And his eyes didn't waver.

"I wanted to check in on you after someone placed the tracker on your car. Figured the most neutral place was out for drinks. Now I'm glad I did."

Eve took her time removing her hand from his grasp. It took only a second for her to miss it. "Well, I'm doing fine. Or I was doing fine. I'm not even sure anymore." Eve's hand migrated to her eyes. She rubbed them, completely forgetting that she had put makeup on that morning.

"Shit," she said as she looked down at the sparkly neutral brown color on her fingertips. She grabbed a napkin and wiped what was left of the eyeshadow off of her fingers. Eve debated checking to see how bad she looked, but also didn't want to draw more attention. "Do I look like a wreck right now?" She gestured to her eyes.

"No. You look beautiful." Eve's eyes jerked back to Kane.

"You look good too. Especially for someone who just saved someone from getting hit by a car."

"Ouch. You wound me. I wanted to talk to you about the tracking device that had been on your car but... I hadn't gotten around to it because of all the excitement from today."

"True. What did you find?"

Kane sighed. "I was hoping to find out more, but it was a standard tracker. Something you could buy online for maybe fifty dollars. I will say it was probably recently put on your car." Kane paused again. "Recently as in the within the last couple of weeks because it still had battery life and these trackers last two to three weeks. I assume they wouldn't have risked trying to get the device off your car to charge it and replace it, but who knows how desperate this person is."

"That makes sense."

Kane tapped his fingers on the table. "There is something else—"

"Is there anything else I can get you guys?" The server appeared again.

"I think we're okay." Eve answered for them both but stared at Kane, waiting to see if he had anything to add.

"Yeah, everything is wonderful over here."

The server took another second to leave, and Eve's attention was drawn back to Kane.

"What were you saying?"

Kane hesitated for a moment. "Ah. Nothing. Wasn't important."

Although Eve's suspicions were raised, she had had enough action for one day. "Would it be rude if I said I wanted to call it a night? Between the adrenaline wearing off and this drink, exhaustion is seeping in. I should also probably contact the girls and let them know what happened."

"Understandable. I'll let the server know, pay the bill, and then I'll walk you home."

Eve thought about telling Kane that wasn't necessary, but she'd be lying to herself. Him walking her home provided a shield in her mind that she thought she needed until she reached her door.

"Does your silence mean that you're gonna fight me on this?"

The Southern lilt that his voice took on when he said those words caused her lips to twitch. "No. Actually, I prefer if you did."

Kane leaned back in his chair and looked around for the server.

Once everything was settled with the bar, Eve and Kane walked to her apartment in silence. When they reached her door, Eve turned to thank him, but Kane's words came out first.

"There's one more thing I want to say. When I figured out that car was coming for you, it scared the shit out of me. I know we don't have the best relationship because of past transgressions—"

Eve sighed. "I don't think I have the energy to talk about that right now."

"I know. I know. But I wanted to get that out into the open."

"Okay. I appreciate you walking me home and saving my life."

"Anytime. Get a good night's sleep, okay?"

"I'll try."

8

"Eve, I think we all would feel safer if you found somewhere else to stay for a while. You have a target on your back. Someone went through the effort of not only tracking your movements every time you get in your car, but they also tried to run you over!" Eve could hear the concern in Rae's voice.

It was a couple of days after the incident near Bar Ten and the women had gathered in Eve's apartment to check on her. It turned into an intervention, and Eve debated with herself whether it had been worth having them over. Although she understood their concern, she didn't know if leaving solved anything besides making her look like a coward.

"You can stay with me if you want," Liv chimed in, having spoken for the first time since Eve filled them in about everything that was happening.

"Listen, if I'm being followed, it makes little sense for me to stay with any of you because it might put you guys in danger too. Also, I don't want any of this hurting anyone's reputation in case it gets bad, especially if it's related to a sitting Member of Congress."

"That's a good point. Then what are you going to do?"

Eve took a second to think about Jules's question before she said, "I have no idea. I wouldn't want to stay with my parents for the same reason that I shouldn't stay with you guys."

"Wait, I know someone who has a home out of town where you might be able to hide."

"Who?" Eve took a sip from her drink and waited for Rae's response. When she got it, her heart and stomach hit the floor.

"Kane."

Eve's heart and stomach hit the floor, and she began to sweat. She recovered from her shock and wiped the back of her hand across her forehead. Eve said, "Rae, you can't go around offering other people's homes."

"What if I say he already talked to Flint about having you stay with him and this was just a warning? He's going to ask you if it's something you want to do?"

Eve's mouth dropped open, and Liv let out a howl of a laugh. When she sobered up a bit, she said, "You stumped her. Well played, Rae. Well played."

Rae turned her attention to Eve. "It's a cute small town based on what Flint described, at least."

"You know I'm a city girl through and through."

"Are we sure this is a good idea?"

"Thanks, Jules, for the thoughtful question. It's not a good idea." Eve stared at the Coke on her table. *Do I still have some rum left? I need something harder than plain soda for this shit here.*

"It's probably the best option you have at the moment. Staying with Kane will a) get you out of town and out of harm's way, and b) would anyone really disapprove of staying with a handsome man alone in the middle of nowhere? I think not."

Eve rolled her eyes at Liv and said, "Then why don't you go with him?"

"I'm not being chased or threatened by an unknown assailant. Nor do I have a history with him. But I'm not going to say I wouldn't treat this as an opportunity to get away for a bit and bang with hardly any interruptions."

Eve closed her eyes, took several deep breaths, and said, "For the millionth time, I'm not going anywhere with Kane, nor are we going to bone. Okay?"

"Famous last words." Liv shrugged and poured another glass of wine.

"Does anyone want to talk about anything else? Literally anything else would be great."

"No, not really."

Although she debated taking one of the pillows on her couch and flinging it at Liv's head, Liv's words made her chuckle. Plus, she couldn't lie to herself and say that she hadn't been thinking about Kane since he came to check things out in her apartment. Some of that was on a professional level, but most of her thoughts were ones she shouldn't be having.

"But on a serious note, Eve, if we can do anything to help, please let us know."

Although the slight bow of her head told the other women in the room that she would, Eve knew that she wouldn't. The less that people knew, the better.

Eve finished cleaning up the glasses from the get-together with her friends. As she was drying her hands from hand washing the glasses they had used, she heard her text message ringtone come from her living room. She strolled into the room and grabbed her phone, which she had haphazardly thrown on her couch moments before she walked into the kitchen. A message from Kane.

Kane: *Hey. How's everything going? Feeling better?*

The conversation she had with her girlfriends earlier popped back into her mind, making her think she knew where this conversation was going.

Eve: *Everything is pretty good and I'm feeling better, thanks for asking.*

Kane: *Great. So, I had an idea that might seem far out there, but would you want to come on a semi-vacation with me?*

Boom. There it was.

Eve: *What do you mean by semi-vacation?*

Kane: *I'm going to be headed home in the next couple of days and thought it would also be a great opportunity for you to get out of the city and away from whoever is trying to hurt you.*

Eve bit her lip while she thought about it for a moment before she typed out a reply.

Eve: *Where would we be going?*

His reply almost caused her to drop her phone.

Kane: *Capitol, VA.*

"Capitol, Virginia… is this a joke?" Phone in hand, Eve darted into her room and scrambled to double-check her notes, causing several pieces of paper to fall off her desk and float to the floor. "Why can't I find the—"

Eve's voice stopped speaking. There, circled in bright red ink, was Capitol, Virginia. She couldn't have predicted the next set of words that flew out from her fingers.

Eve: Sure. I'll come with you to Capitol.

"IS THIS EVERYTHING?"

Eve looked down at the two suitcases and book bag she had packed and yawned. The cool, crisp air did little to wake her up when she so desperately wanted to sleep. Why on earth had they decided that this time of morning was a great time to leave? "Yes?"

"I assumed you would have more bags."

"Now, now, you know what they say when you assume." She walked around to the passenger door that Kane had opened for her. Once she had climbed in the large, dark SUV, he closed the door and headed to the trunk. She set her book bag at her feet before turning her body to look at him and wait. Eve smirked when he realized how much heavier the bags were than they looked, but she wasn't surprised when he had no problem lifting the suitcases one by one into the car.

She maneuvered her body to face forward again and a familiar smell tickled her nostrils. She noticed that there were two coffees sitting in the center console. At that point, Kane opened the door and slid his body into the driver's seat.

"Is one of these for me?"

Kane nodded before looking in his rearview mirror. "The one up front. There are also some croissants in the bag near your feet."

She grabbed the cup without thinking about it and took a long sip of the liquid that helped fuel people all over the world. Eve could have danced in her seat as the warm coffee flowed through her body, helping her to feel more alive after such an early wake-up call. Her body was not built for getting up at 5:00 a.m. She grabbed the bag near her feet and took a peek inside. "Thank you so much. I hope it wasn't too far out of your way to get it."

"Wasn't a problem at all. Are you ready to get going?"

"Sure. Let's hit the road."

With that, Kane started the vehicle and the two were on their way to Capitol, Virginia.

They spent the first thirty minutes of the car ride in a peaceful silence. Although Eve had expected any silence to be awkward, this wasn't. She was enjoying Kane's company, even if they weren't saying anything at all.

"I need to tell you some things about Capitol." And there was the end to the silence. On one hand, she was grateful that he was talking again because it meant less time she had to spend with her thoughts. On the other hand, she was a little nervous because this would be the longest amount of time spent with him outside of when they hung out with their mutual friends.

"Go on."

"I'm sure you've done your research, but Capitol isn't anything like Washington, D.C."

"I figured as much."

"Capitol is a small town where everyone knows everyone. Most of the people have family that have lived there for generations. I'm one of the few people who left town and then didn't officially return."

His word choice led Eve to raise an eyebrow. Although she wanted to act ambivalent, she was genuinely curious. "What do you mean officially?"

"I bought a house in Capitol."

"Wait. Let me make sure I am understanding you correctly. You have a house in Capitol and rent an apartment in D.C. Am I getting that right?"

Kane nodded, but didn't expand further. Eve continued her questioning. "Why not just move back to Capitol?"

"My goal is to move back home eventually. But I still have things I want to do in D.C." This time, he glanced at her for what seemed longer than necessary before turning his attention back to the road. "Plus, it would be harder to attend meetings for the foundation in D.C."

"I mean, it would be a long commute but also not unheard of. Well, I guess it depends on how many meetings you attend in D.C."

Kane shrugged his shoulders but said nothing else. Eve debated with herself whether it was worth probing him further. *Well, I have nothing to lose. Might as well try a bit of a fresh approach.* "What else can you tell me about Capitol?"

"Many people are going to want to know everything about you. And I mean everything. Most of the town knows who was seen with whom, or who was doing what. News travels quick in Capitol, so be careful if you don't want something to be known. The folks in this town have a funny way of getting information out one way or another."

Eve made a mental note to keep the real reason she was traveling to Capitol to herself at all costs. She couldn't afford to let that get out. "Anything else I should know about?"

"People are gonna be very curious about you, being that you didn't grow up in Capitol and all."

"That's understandable, given how small of a town it is. Can you tell me anything about your family? What are they like?"

Kane paused for a moment as he switched lanes. He spoke again once he had safely moved around a slower car in his lane. "My mom, grandma, and siblings all still live in Capitol. My mom owns one of the local diners in town; that was left to her by my grandfather. My grandma owns the hair salon. Some people she has served over the years have been true characters. That reminds me, if you don't want anything shared with half of the town, don't tell Sofia and Stella."

"Would they leak it faster than you can say secret?"

Kane smirked in her direction and nodded. "They caught me kissing a girl my junior year of high school and Ma knew about it before I could step foot over the threshold. Not that she was angry or anything." Eve laughed, and Kane continued. "Anyway, my grandparents knew each other in passing but officially met and began talking because my grandma was working in the hair salon, so it holds a special place in our family's heart."

When Kane said nothing else, Eve gestured for him to continue. This conversation made a wonderful addition to the coffee she was drinking.

"Grandpa came into the salon for a haircut just when Grandma was starting out. Apparently, they had seen each other in passing over the years, but Grandpa had come back home to take over ownership of the diner after my great-grandfather wanted to retire. It was love at first sight."

Eve smiled in Kane's direction, enjoying the fact that he

was sharing parts of himself with her. That smile quickly turned into a frown because she didn't know if she wanted to know more about him. At one point she had the desire, but that was squashed when he left her alone in her bed after they had spent the night together. "Sounds like they had the storybook romance."

Kane glanced at her before turning his eyes back to the road. "I guess you could say that."

"Are they still together?"

"My grandfather died a couple years back. It was devastating to everyone, especially my grandmother. But she's doing well and thriving, so that's the best I can hope for."

Eve silently agreed and took a sip of her coffee. When she swallowed, she asked, "Is there anything else I should know about your family?"

"My mom took over the diner when Grandpa died and has been running it ever since. My dad is a truck driver, so he's gone for longer periods of time. He talks about retiring, but who knows what will happen."

"Your siblings?"

"Hensley is my younger sister, and Axel is my younger brother. Hensley owns a bakery and Axel is the sheriff."

Eve had no more questions so, when Kane finished talking, she stared out the window and watched the sunrise cast a warm glow on the fields and trees as they drove past. After a few moments, Eve was the one to break their comfortable silence.

"You know, I'm a little nervous about going to Capitol."

"I can see why you would be but tell me."

"I'm not nervous when I go to congressional offices and talk to congressional members. I'm usually not nervous when

I talk to someone on phone to try to get a story. But most of that takes place in D.C. and, outside of college, that's the only place I've been for a long period of time. This is an unfamiliar environment where I'm a complete stranger and I'm a little worried I won't be liked? Normally, that is the first thing on my mind." Eve tapped her fingernails on her phone, which she was balancing on her lap. "I think it's a mixture of everything that has happened plus going to an unknown town."

"I get that. I felt the same way when I left because I want to become a Marine." Kane reached over and patted Eve's hand before placing his hand back on the steering wheel. "If anyone gives you any trouble, just let me know."

"Kane, I can handle myself."

"I know you can. I'm just saying you don't have to go out alone."

His words hung in the car as silence once again saved them from saying things that might be too much for the other to handle. Eve turned her attention back to staring out her window at the foliage. There was so much that should be said, but that could wait for another day.

9

———

"Eve."

She could hear the voice in the distance, but her eyelids felt as if they had boulders keeping them shut. She heard the same voice call her name again, but she still couldn't open her eyes.

A warm hand touched hers and gave it a gentle squeeze. Her eyelids fluttered but the urge to keep her eyes closed was still there. When she was more awake, her eyes tried to focus on the first thing she saw—Kane's hand on hers.

"Hey," she said. As soon as the word left her mouth, a yawn threatened to escape, leading her to fling her other hand up to her mouth to cover it.

"Hey, yourself. Looks like you fell asleep over there."

"Yeah, that's what happens when I'm forced to wake up too early."

"Could it have also been due to the fact that I'm an excellent driver and the car lulled you to sleep?"

Eve shrugged. "I guess." She looked around and out the window. "Are we getting close?"

Kane nodded. "We're a couple miles away. Thought you might want to be awake when we entered Capitol. There's something I want you see."

Eve grinned at the thoughtful gesture, and her eyes were firmly planted on the window. A few minutes later, the car drove up to a welcome sign and Eve belly laughed. The sign read, "Welcome to Capitol. No, not that capitol. The other one."

"Is that serious?" she asked, trying to contain her laughter but failing.

"Yep. Can't say this town doesn't have a sense of humor."

The welcome sign brought a sense of ease to the pit of Eve's stomach. Maybe her time in Capitol wouldn't be so bad after all.

"There's one thing that I forgot to tell you."

"Uh-oh. What is it?"

"Watch out for my grandma."

"Wait, what?"

"My grandma, although I love her dearly, is somewhat known as the town's matchmaker. She has made it her mission to help people find their soulmates. This is not to say she isn't successful, but some of the results have been comical to say the least."

Eve couldn't stop the smile that was playing on the corners of her lips. "She sounds amazing." She could see that Kane was also fighting a grin, too, although she bet that she couldn't get him to admit it.

Eve and Kane drove through town, and Eve noted some places she wanted to visit while she was here.

"I'll give you a proper tour of Capitol once we're settled."

"Sounds good."

What Eve could see painted a picture of a charming small town. One that you might see in a Hallmark holiday movie. Well, without the snow and holiday cheer, because that season had passed.

"Is this Capitol's shopping center?" Eve asked as the SUV drove passed a ton of storefronts on one block.

"Yes, it is. In fact, my sister's bakery is on this strip." Kane glanced out of his window before turning his head back to the road. "Looks like we passed it already. Sorry I should have mentioned it sooner."

"That's okay. I'm sure I'll see it while we are here."

Their drive continued for a few more minutes before Eve notice a building that piqued her interest. "Is that one of Capitol's schools?"

"Yep. That's our high school. What happened in those walls, stays in those walls."

"Oh, really?" Eve said, stealing a look at Kane. "Now you can't say that and not elaborate."

"Yes, I can."

"No. You can't."

"Yes."

"No."

Eve shook her head and laughed at their back and forth. Some of the nerves that were still floating through her body lessen. "Okay, you won this battle, but you haven't won the war." Eve glanced at him once more and saw a small smile appeared on his lips, but he said nothing more.

A minute later, Eve watched as the buildings became more residential, signaling that maybe they were getting closer to Kane's home. A lot of the houses they drove past were colonial style and farmhouse style, each with its own unique character and charm. Soon Kane's vehicle pulled up to a cream-colored farmhouse with a red mailbox close to the road. He turned down the driveway and pulled up to the front of the house.

When Kane put the SUV in park, he cast a small smile at Eve and hopped out of the car. Eve took her time grabbing her book bag and her phone and looked up when Kane opened the passenger door. The first thing she noticed when she stepped out of the car was how quiet it was. His closest neighbor had to be at least a half a mile, if not more, down the road.

"This is beautiful," Eve said. She knew that her mouth was slightly open in amazement, but she didn't care.

"Thanks. I'll open the door for you and then grab our bags."

"Oh, wait. Let me grab this." Eve turned back to the car, opened the passenger side door, and grabbed the remnants of the food they'd had earlier and the empty coffee cups. With that, she followed Kane up the porch stairs and waited for him to unlock the door.

"Welcome to my home." Eve stepped around Kane and entered the house. The first thing she noticed was the staircase leading upstairs. She watched as Kane took off his shoes and followed suit, neatly placing her boots near his. She followed him as he entered his living room and was amazed by what she saw. The thoughts that had crossed her mind about what she thought his house might look like vanished as he gave her a tour of his sanctuary. The neutral to dark colors fitted what she knew of Kane's personality to a tee.

The house's exterior didn't match what she'd imagined. The whole farmhouse aesthetic stopped at the front door; his space had been completely renovated to include more high-tech gadgets than anything else as far as she could see. There was a digital thermostat on the wall and, excitedly, he showed her that he could control the lights in the room using his phone. The space included some rustic touches, including exposed dark brown beams on the ceiling, but overall the home seemed to be more modern than she was expecting. "Although I've seen only a small part of your home, I can already tell this is homier than your apartment in D.C." She looked at some photos he had on the walls of who she assumed to be family and friends. The smiling faces and their prominent placement told her that his family meant a lot to him. Or that another family member wanted to make sure he didn't forget any of them.

"Funny you should say that." He grabbed the trash that she was carrying.

"Oh yeah?" Eve leaned back on her heels and waited for him to continue.

"D.C. never really felt like home. I have the basics that I need to survive, but my heart has always been in this Capitol. Not that one."

Eve snorted, but she was happy that he was willing to open up a bit, especially since they would be living together for however much time it took for the threat against her to be taken care of. But she felt a small pang in her stomach that she didn't want to take the time to dissect. Kane announcing his plans to move away from D.C. when she did not intend to do so had caused it. But why did she care?

"Shall we continue?"

His words pulled Eve out of her head and she said, "After you."

The two finished touring the first level and made their way back to their bags. Kane picked up Eve's suitcases as Eve grabbed her book bag and the two walked up the stairs to the second floor. Kane showed her the first of two guest rooms. It was a nice size and had a full-size bed, a dresser, and a ceiling fan.

"I figured it made sense for you to stay in the guest room across the hall from me because it's bigger, but if you don't want to, you're welcome to stay in here. Or, hell, in my bedroom for that matter."

"And where will you stay if I take your bed?"

"I think you already know the answer to that." His voice dropped an octave as he took a small step closer to her. The heat from his gaze unnerved her, but she did her best to not let him know it. Liv's words about having sex with him again floated back to the surface. Part of her knew it was a bad idea, but the other part didn't care.

"Can you show me where my room is?"

Eve's words must have broken the spell Kane had put them both under because he backed up and moved his eyes away from hers. He led the way down the hall.

"Here's my room and here's yours," he said, gesturing to both spaces. He opened the door that led to the room that he thought she would like, and she smiled. He had been right on the money with that assumption.

The queen-size bed took up more space in the room, but there was still plenty of space for her to maneuver around. The theme of the room was light neutral colors, which included a beige and white comforter on the bed. There was also a drawer and two smaller nightstands with lamps on either side. Eve watched as Kane walked over to the closet and opened the door.

"Nice size closet," she mumbled, thinking about how she could make this room more her own.

"Is there anything you can think of that you might need immediately?"

Eve shook her head and placed her book bag down near one of the room's windows. She stared outside for a moment, thinking about Representative Blake, before Kane's words brought her back to the present.

"What are you thinking about?"

"Uh, just wondering where I can set up a workstation. I might work at the kitchen counter or in the living room—"

"I have a study in the basement. I'll show you once you finish getting settled."

Eve nodded her head. "Sounds good." She kneeled down and dug into her book bag.

"Think you'll be ready to go in about twenty to thirty minutes?"

Eve stopped digging and turned to look up at Kane. "Where are we going?"

"Supermarket. There's no food in here. Well, none that's good anyway. Thought it would be easier for you to come with, but if you want to make a list of things you'd like to eat, that also works. I can always go back if necessary."

Eve thought for a second before deciding. "I can go with you to the supermarket. Maybe we'll run into some people who'll tell me embarrassing stories about you."

She chuckled at the playful look he gave her. "You think I'm being funny. But you know it's going to happen."

"THAT'S PROBABLY the only time I've seen him turn beet red. And I've known him all my life. But you know what made it better? It happened while he was in high school when he was mean to both of us."

"Axel." That one word served as a warning from Kane, but all it did was make the man she had just met laugh.

"Don't worry. He's much better now." Hensley said, before poking Kane on his shoulder.

Eve couldn't fight the smile that was making its way across her face. She had spoken this interaction into existence because, halfway through their shopping trip, they ran into Kane's younger brother, Axel, and sister, Hensley. There was no doubting that Axel and Kane were related. From their broad shoulders, to their cheekbones that could have been carved in marble. Their hazel eyes had a hint of playfulness in them. But whereas Kane's hair was longer and shaggier, Axel kept his hair cut shorter, just a hint longer than Kane's hair cut when he was a Marine. Hensley, on the other hand, had hair long enough to throw into a messy bun and her brown eyes weren't too far off from her older siblings'.

Kane was more on the quiet side unless spoken to, but his brother and sister were the exact opposite. They had no problem engaging in conversation. Eve could see that his sister was trying to dig for information about her. All of her answers would be reported back to the entire town in no time flat.

"While Axel continues to blabber on about nothing, Eve, I think we'd both like to know more about you. What do you do? Are you from D.C.? How'd you meet Kane? How long have you known each other?"

"Hensley, could you ask any more questions? Maybe you should move into journalism like Eve."

Eve chuckled at the sibling banter, having not experienced it because she was an only child. "I'm from Washington, D.C. I left to go away to college but came back as soon as I graduated. I work for the *Capitol Express* in D.C."

"I can only imagine the stories you work on."

"Oh, if you only knew." And Eve meant every word.

"You know Ma's going to want to have a word with you since you came back into town and didn't tell her you were coming."

Eve's attention was drawn back to Kane's brother as he uttered those words. This could be good.

"We'll stop by the diner before heading home. I assume she's there?"

Both siblings nodded their heads.

"Well, we should probably wrap this up and head over. I'll see you guys later." Kane started walking down the aisle with Eve following behind him. Kane stopped suddenly and turned back to his siblings, who were still standing there. "Is there any chance that you two will keep your traps shut until I get there?"

Eve chuckled when Axel nodded his head as his sister shook hers. "I figured as much."

"Wait, before you leave, Eve, you and I should trade numbers in case you want to hang out with someone whose name doesn't rhyme with *bane*. You know as in the bane of my existence?"

"You're hilarious," Kane said as Eve pulled out her phone.

The women traded numbers and Kane reminded the group that they needed to be on their way.

"Kane."

Kane turned around and faced his sister.

"Have fun seeing Ma."

10

———

"Kane, why didn't you tell me you were coming home?"

Eve turned to the sound of the voice and found an older woman standing in front of them. Her long salt-and-pepper hair was pulled back in a ponytail and she wore a light blue T-shirt and a dark pair of denim jeans. The T-shirt had *Capitol Diner* written across the chest in white letters. A smile lit up Kane's face as he met the woman halfway. Their embrace lasted a few seconds and the woman placed her hands on his cheeks.

"You look great, Kane. Still doesn't explain why you didn't tell me were on your way here."

"Couldn't it be a surprise?"

"With you? No."

Kane's hands flew up to heart. "Ma, you wound me." His words took on even more of a Southern lilt, which Eve attributed to being back home.

Eve smirked at the interaction in front of her. Their

happiness radiated off of them like the sun's rays off of the hot asphalt in the middle of summer. The woman turned to Eve and smiled before she threw a glare at her son.

"Ma, this is Eve. Eve, this is my mother, Lori."

Eve hesitated for a moment before holding her hand out to shake Lori's. Lori looked down at Eve's hand before looking back up at her. "We greet with hugs 'round here." Eve stepped into her embrace and a sense of comfort flowed over her skin. Lori leaned back after several seconds and gave Eve a big smile. "Why don't y'all stay for lunch?" Her eyes moved from Eve's to Kane's and back to Eve's, seeking confirmation.

"Ma, we have groceries in the car and—"

"Bring the perishables in here and we'll store them properly. Lunch will be on the house."

Based on the shifting of his eyes, Eve could tell that this made Kane uncomfortable. "I have no problem paying for our meal."

Lori patted her son on the shoulder. "I know you can but it's rare that I can spoil my eldest so let me." Not waiting for an answer, she led Eve and Kane to a booth and handed the two of them some menus from a holder on the table. "Pick anything and we'll make it for ya. I'll give you a moment to decide." With that, Lori left Eve and Kane to read the menu.

"Is there anything you recommend?" All the food on the menu looked delicious, and Eve knew that there was no way she'd be able to decide what to eat on her own.

"Depends on what you're in the mood for. I love the shrimp and grits and the fried chicken, mac 'n' cheese, and greens."

Kane's words and the pictures she was staring at made her mouth water. "I'll do the shrimp and grits."

"Picking the Southern fried chicken and waffles. Because why not?"

Eve agreed. Why not?

"Have you decided what you want to eat?" Lori asked as she strolled over to their table. The two rattled off their orders.

"Ma, could you come have lunch with us?"

Lori thought for a moment. "I have a couple of things to finish up, but I'll be back when your food is ready, and we can chat."

Lori walked away and Kane ran a hand through his brown hair. Seeing him with longer hair still tripped Eve up. When Kane had stormed back into Eve's life through helping salvage Rae's moving day over a year ago, his new, longer locks had surprised her. Well, him being there period took her by surprise, if she had to be honest with herself.

"Are you enjoying yourself so far?"

The question caught Eve off guard. Normally she was the one doing the interviewing. "Yeah. This usually isn't my scene, but Capitol seems to be cool and has a lot of charm."

"What do you mean it's 'not your scene'?" Kane smiled at his mother when she walked over and set waters in front of them.

"This is not from a place of judgment, but I've spent most of my time in the city. That being said, I have spent little time in Capitol, so I'm excited to learn more about everything." Only she understood the double meaning of her statement. She wanted to explore Capitol, but she also intended to get to the bottom of the Representative Blake story. "You definitely seem more at ease here, which makes sense."

"Yeah. It feels good to be home." Kane paused for a second. "Eve?"

Eve's eyes made their way back to Kane's. His words had stopped her people watching. "Yes?"

"I'm glad you came out here with me. At first it felt weird given... our history, but hopefully this is a relaxing experience."

"I hope so too. I brought a bunch of work I need to finish up, so I'll need time to get that done." After she told her boss she'd almost gotten hit by a car and that she was going to Representative Blake's hometown, the *Capitol Express* had cleared Eve to travel to Capitol to continue her investigative reporting.

The two continued their small talk until Lori brought their dishes out from the kitchen and set their meals in front of them. "I need to run to the back and get something. I'll be right back." With that, she left the duo, who greedily dug into their meals.

"Kane." Eve finished chewing her food. "This is amazing."

"I wouldn't steer you wrong."

Eve glanced up at him and saw that his eyes were trained on her. The tone of his voice led her to think there was a double meaning there.

"Sorry about that. I wanted to grab a glass of water for myself. Everything okay?"

Eve looked up and smiled at Lori. "This is so good. I didn't realize how hungry I was until I started eating."

"Ma, I don't even know why you ask. You know the food is always great."

"Because it's polite." She shared a small smile with her son before turning her attention to Eve. "So, Eve, you're from

D.C. originally? Oh, wait, I shouldn't be talking to you while you're eating, but I'm so excited. Kane never brings a woman home to meet us."

Eve could stop her lips from twitching. Her gaze landed on Kane, who was staring at his mother. "Oh, no. Kane and I aren't dating. We're just..." Eve tried to find the word to describe their relationship. "Friends."

Kane broke the stare and turned to Eve. She couldn't read his expression.

"She's staying with me temporarily. A small vacation away from the city." Well, he wasn't wrong.

"Ah. Well, I hope you enjoy your time in Capitol. Depending on how long you stay, we have several activities going on." She paused before jumping a bit in her chair. "You'll be here for the barbecue we're having next week. A bunch of folks in town are coming and it should be great. You'll both still be here, right?"

Eve and Kane hadn't established how long they were planning to stay in Capitol. But being in town for at least a week made sense.

"It sounds exciting and, yes, I think we'll be here for at least a week. Since this is a party, can I bring anything?"

"That's so kind of you. No, we should have everything we need."

"Lori, we need you in the back." A server interrupted their lovely conversation.

Lori took another sip from her glass of water and stood up. "Well, it was nice meeting you, Eve. I know I'll see you around. Kane, I expect that you'll try to be social while you're here, so I guess I'll see you around too."

Kane chuckled and Lori waved before she headed to the

back. The couple finished their meal and Eve groaned. "I think I ate way too much. You might have to roll me out of here."

"I don't know about rolling you out, but I can carry you." He stood up and based on his stance, Eve could tell that he wasn't kidding.

Although she really didn't want to, Eve used every ounce of strength to stand up and she turned around to find Kane pulling out some bills from his wallet.

"Did your mom even bring us a bill?"

Kane gave her a smirk. "I caught how much our meals cost when we were looking for the menu, then I estimated the tip and taxes. I put more down than necessary, but it's fine."

"Your mom's gonna have some choice words for you." Eve said in a singsong voice.

"Eh. It's not like I haven't heard it before."

She knew the wink that Kane sent her way was meant in jest, but she couldn't stop the tingly feeling it gave her. Was she overthinking all of this based on a wink?

"Kane, didn't know you were back in town."

Eve and Kane turned around in unison and found an older man standing behind them.

He was shorter than Eve by a couple of inches but his hair was a familiar blond color, although it was starting to go grey. He was dressed in dark red polo and black slacks. The man held out his hand to shake Kane's and then Eve's before continuing. "I'm Mayor Blake. Welcome to Capitol." Something about the way his eyes were hyper focused on her, Eve made sure to not break the eye contact. It was something she typically used while interviewing politicians at home and her instincts kicked in. Although she had just met the man something didn't sit right with her.

Eve's heart skipped a beat at his introduction. "Thanks. I'm Eve, originally from D.C."

"Oh, really? My son and his wife live there. He represents our great district in Congress."

"Are you Representative Anthony Blake's father?" Eve figured hiding most of what she knew about Representative Blake was wise here. She didn't want to alert Kane or Mayor Blake to any suspicions that she might have. When he nodded, she added, "Ah. I've heard of him."

She debated expanding her answer further, but figured it made sense to not draw attention to how she knew him. His eyes didn't stray from their intended target, which just so happened to be her. She felt Kane move slightly closer to her and wondered if he was sensing the same thing she was. Knowing that he was close by eased some of the tension she felt building in her mind. Which caused a whole slew of other feelings that she really didn't want to dissect at this moment.

"How long are you staying in town?" Mayor Blake's eyes finally veered from Eve to Kane.

"As long as we want. We don't have a set timeline." Kane said, answering for the both of them. Technically that was true, and she was happy that he seemed to be as flexible to a timeframe as she was. Also was it weird that his question made her even more suspicious?

"Kane! You forgot your groceries." Lori came over with several bags and handed them over to her eldest. "Good afternoon, Mayor Blake. Staying for lunch? I can seat you." Mayor

Blake nodded once more and followed Lori to a table. Eve let out a breath she didn't know she was holding. She followed the mayor with her eyes, betting he would go to the ends of the earth to protect his son.

"Shall we go?"

"Sounds good."

IT TOOK no time for Eve and Kane to arrive back at his home. The duo grabbed the bags of food out of Kane's truck and brought them into the kitchen. Eve was unloading one of the bags she brought in when Kane's words stopped her.

"How about I unpack the groceries and you can unpack your things?"

"That sounds like a good idea." She stepped back and brushed her hands across her denim-covered thighs. "I'll be upstairs, I guess."

Kane gave her a small smile before turning back to the groceries.

Eve headed upstairs to the room that would be hers during their time in Capitol. She unpacked her clothes and placed them in the dresser and then unpacked her toiletries. Once she had her items where she wanted them, she figured now was the perfect the time to take a shower since she hadn't had the opportunity that morning.

"Kane?"

Her question was met by silence, so she walked out into the hallway and called his name once more.

"Yeah?" His voice sounded far away.

"Where are your towels?"

"What?" Was he on the first level?

She huffed at his response, realizing that he couldn't hear her. She bounded down the stairs and took a quick look around, but still didn't see Kane. "Where are you?"

"In my study," came the still-muffled voice. She headed down the next flight of stairs into the basement. She reached the door he'd shown her earlier and knocked before turning the doorknob. Eve peered around the door and came face-to-face with Kane, whose eyes were glued to his computer monitor.

"Hey, I wanted to know where your towels were. I was hoping to take a shower."

He pushed his computer chair away from his desk. "I can grab one for you."

"Oh, don't worry about it. Just tell me where they are, and I can grab them myself. You look busy." She shifted her body to see if she might see what he was working on, but he closed the window.

"This is nothing." His eyes moved away from the monitor to look at her. Something was up.

"Are you sure? Anything I can help with? Is it related to the foundation?"

"No, it's not, and right now I don't need any help, but I'll let you know if I do." He cleared his throat. "The towels are in the closet to the left of my bedroom."

"Ah. Okay. Thanks," Eve said. "Oh, by the way, I totally forgot to grab my soda from the grocery store, but don't worry about it."

"You sure?"

"Yep. I'll be fine without it." She gave him a small wave before she left and closed the door behind her.

"Let me know if you need anything else!" he called after her.

Whatever he was working on sure didn't look like nothing.

11

——————

A couple of days later, the pinging of Eve's phone brought her out of the work she was doing. Well, the work that she should have been doing... For the better part of the last hour she had gone down several rabbit holes while she was supposed to be doing research. There were some days when these rabbit holes would bring forth helpful information, but this was not one of those days. Eve grabbed her phone and saw that it was a message from Jules.

Jules: *Want to do a group video call in about ten minutes?*

Eve almost declined her offer, but a glance at the clock on her computer told her it was way past time for her to stop working on the article. It helped that she was further ahead than usual, probably due to the fact that she didn't have as many distractions in Capitol as she did at home.

Eve: *That works for me. Is everyone else joining? Same app we usually use?*

Jules: *Yep. Talk to you in a few.*

Eve figured she had just enough time to use the bathroom and grab a bottle of one of her favorite beers that she had insisted Kane get for her when he made a second trip to the grocery store.

She rushed downstairs and ran into a hard, warm body. The only thing that kept her from falling to the ground was the grip that Kane's hands had on her waist. Her eyes wandered from his chest up to his face, where a smile played on his lips.

"Going somewhere fast?"

"Um." Eve took a second to collect herself, shifting her thoughts away from what might be a better use of his hands. She took a step back. "Rae, Jules, and Liv wanted to video chat, so I was just grabbing a beer to get ready."

"I'm almost about done with dinner. I'll come up and let you know when it's ready?"

Eve gave him a slight nod as her thoughts drifted toward how they seemed to fall into a rhythm. So far, they alternated who cooked dinner and washed dishes. Even had an argument over who got to pick the show they wanted to watch last night. They laughed about it afterward, but still it sent her thoughts swirling.

"Eve."

"Sorry. Yeah, just yell and I'll be ready." She moved out of his arms and headed over to the fridge. She pulled the door open, found the bottle she was looking for, and turned back to Kane. "Also sorry about running into you."

"It's fine. No harm, no foul."

Eve headed out of the kitchen when she heard Kane call her name.

"You don't ever have to apologize for getting that close to me."

WHILE SHE WAS WAITING for the app to open, she took a swig of her beer. Eve sat back and thought about how thankful she was for the ability to connect virtually. Having the ability to have a little piece of home was super special to her, and it did wonders when she was missing home. She made a note to check in on her parents later that evening to make sure that everything was okay with them as well. As she was about to place the bottle next to her laptop, three familiar faces popped up on her screen.

"Hey!" Liv's boisterous voice was the first thing she heard. She didn't realize how much she missed them until that moment. No happy hours, barre classes, no drunken movie nights for the foreseeable future.

"Hi!" Rae responded. "We all met up yesterday, so this call is about you."

"Thanks, guys. Way to rub it in."

"We didn't mean it that way. We missed you and figured a video call was the next best thing."

"Well before I start talking, can y'all give me a rundown about what is going on with you since I'm out of the loop?"

The women took turns informing her about what was going on in their lives. Liv was busy with wedding season ramping back up; there was nothing new in Jules' life besides her work on the family foundation's communications team. Rae still was adjusting to Flint's new schedule as a congressman, while also working and fixing up their new home rental.

"How are you? How is Capitol treating you?" Jules asked, ready to get to the heart of their call.

"Not too bad. Everyone is super friendly. Well, almost everyone."

"Keep going," Jules prompted with a sip of her wine.

"I got some weird vibes from the mayor, but I don't have much to base that on." Eve retold her run-in with mayor.

"Interesting. Do you think he might know the real reason you left D.C. to go to Capitol?"

Eve shrugged. Not even her friends knew the whole reason why she came to Capitol.

"It wouldn't hurt to look into him as well then." Even as Jules said the words, her gaze was fixed somewhere off camera.

Eve nodded but didn't tell the group that was on her agenda; she took a sip of her beer instead.

"Speaking of Capitol, how's it going living with Mr. Kane Slade?"

Clank. Eve knew the noise came from her dropping her beer back on the desk harder than she intended. A quick glance at the doorway confirmed that Kane was still in the kitchen and she was thankful that he hadn't come up to tell her that dinner was ready. She knew it was only a matter of time before that question came up.

"It's fine. Just like having a roommate."

"You haven't boned yet?"

"Liv! Right now, is not the time." Rae rolled her eyes.

"When is it not the right time to ask about boning? Asking for a friend."

Eve couldn't control the snort as she shook her head. "We haven't, as you so eloquently put it, boned."

"Why are you talking to us then? Get to it."

"Sounds like someone else needs to get some and is projecting."

"Hey, dinner is—"

Eve looked over at Kane, whose words died on his lips. He looked as if he hadn't been expecting her to be on a video call.

"He cooks too?" Liv's attempt at whispering failed, and the snort that Rae let out caused Jules to giggle.

"Maybe I threw the meal in the oven and Kane was telling me the timer went off."

Liv raised an eyebrow and asked, "Is that what happened?"

"No, but—"

"Aha! So, he cooked the meal."

"He did, but—"

"Have fun at dinner." Liv's smile turned almost sinister before she gave a small wave and signed off. Rae and Jules laughed at the demonstration before saying their goodbyes and signing off too.

"Do I even want to know?"

Eve turned to Kane and shrugged. "Probably not."

She followed Kane downstairs and found that he had grilled two steaks and cooked mashed potatoes and spinach. Everything was already on their plates and sitting on the counter.

"I didn't know what you wanted to drink."

"That's fine. I'll grab a glass of water. Do you want a beer?" Eve brushed past him and her hand touched his.

Although it was innocent, the small contact between the two of them jolted her body. Not from being scared or angry, but from excitement that was unexpected.

Kane nodded before reaching into a cabinet to get a glass for her.

"I'll bring the drinks and you can bring dinner?"

Kane dipped his head once more and picked up the plates as Eve walked over to his fridge to fill her glass. She joined him in the dining room and set the beer in front of him.

"Thanks," he said as she sat down to eat.

"So how was your day?" Eve asked before putting a piece of steak in her mouth. Kane's eyes were locked on her as chewed the meat. The steak tasted like heaven in her mouth. "Wow, this is delicious, by the way."

She watched as a small smile appeared on his face. Was he nervous about her reaction to the meal? "Thank you. My day was quiet. Did a bit of this and a bit of that. You?"

Kane's answer made Eve raise an eyebrow. His reaction when she entered his study the day she'd arrived, plus his answer now, further raised the questions that were floating through Eve's mind. He could have easily dodged the question by saying he was working on things for the foundation, but he didn't.

"Mostly catching up on things for work. We finished interviewing all the freshmen congressional members, but I'm working on a few articles and projects from here." She could be evasive too. "I wanted to ask you something though."

Kane glanced up from his plate. "What do you want to know?"

"Did anything big happen fifteen to twenty years ago in town?"

"What do you mean, something big?"

"Scandal wise." Eve knew that her questioning opened the door to more questions, but she needed something to go on.

"Let's see... I would have been in high school or so?" Kane paused for a moment as his hand flew to his lips. She watched his movements as he became more lost in thought. She didn't want to disturb him. "The only thing I can really think of is that there was a hit and run that never got solved."

Eve tried to hide her surprise but failed. "Please tell me the person who got hit is okay now."

"Yes. Well, I shouldn't answer for Abbie because I'm not sure, but she survived if that's what you mean."

Eve took a deep breath and blew the air out. "Thank goodness."

"Yeah. The town was pretty shaken up about the whole thing. Came together to help her and her family out and everything."

"So, you mentioned that the police never solved the case?"

Kane nodded his head. "I think they left the case open, but everyone assumed it was someone who wasn't from the area."

The wheels in Eve's head were rolling as she put the potential pieces together. She needed to do some digging into this hit and run.

Although she wanted to tell Kane, she hesitated. She didn't have a reason to not trust him, but thoughts of what Rae had mentioned—about Kane's secret projects and him volunteering to help both Rae and Flint when they were in trouble—swirled. Rae mentioned that Kane was away on a few occasions when the whole group had gotten together; it wasn't that it was uncommon for him to be away, it was the mysterious air that surrounded it that made Eve suspicious. He was never on vacation or gone on a work trip. He was just "away." All of this made her wonder: What was Kane hiding, and was she doing the right thing by keeping this from him?

12

Eve grabbed her phone, rescuing her ears from the sound; she had another message. She was several days into her stay in Capitol and, since she wasn't in D.C. anymore, the phone calls and messages had lessened. She mostly heard from her parents, whom she had to tell somewhat of a white lie in order to avoid too many questions about why she skipped town, and her friends, with messages here and there from work.

Hensley: Hey!

Hensley: Want to get out of the house for a bit?

Eve looked around and figured she wasn't doing anything, so why not?

Eve: Sure. When do you want to meet up?

Hensley: Would thirty minutes be okay?

Eve: Sounds good.

Eve was ready to go with plenty of time to spare. She sent Kane a quick text letting him know she was going to hang out with his sister, and they were off.

"I just need to bring this bag to my mom. She asked me to meet her at the hair salon. Shouldn't take long at all."

Although Eve hadn't known Hensley for very long, nor had she been in town very long, she suspected that this wouldn't be a fast trip. Eve fiddled around on her phone for what seemed like an hour with no sign of Hensley returning. It had only been fifteen minutes.

With a huff, Eve exited the car and locked the doors. Although they were in a small town where everyone knew everyone, her instincts told her it was probably wise to lock the doors anyway. Or maybe that was city living infused in her brain. She opened the door of the salon and was greeted by loud chattering and laughter. The sounds of glee came to a halt when a woman realized that someone else had entered. Eve surveyed the room quickly but didn't find Hensley or Lori.

The salon was decorated in bold colors and photos of people with exquisite hairstyles. The salon was the definition of a bright spot in this small town.

"Are you Eve?" The question came from one of the hair stylists who had just finished rinsing a woman's hair out. Her gray hair had streaks of blue in it, which felt right at home with the decor of the salon. She wore her long hair in a pony-tail, probably to keep the strands from getting in her way while she worked.

"Yes, I am." Although Eve was used to talking to strangers, the number of eyes in the room that were staring at her made her uneasy.

"Welcome to Capitol! I'm Rose and I'm Kane's grand-mother. I'd give you a hug, but I need to get Mindy here over to my chair. Mindy, right this way." She helped the woman move from the washing sink to a styling chair and prepared to continue doing her hair. "If you're looking for Hensley and Lori, they stepped into the back to grab something but should be out shortly." With that, the chatter in the salon resumed and Eve's appearance didn't seem to matter much. Anyone could see that the people in the salon had known each other for many years. Based on the things that Kane told her before they arrived, it was more than likely that her hanging out with Hensley would cause the gossip crew's tongues to wag.

"Sounds good. Is it okay if I sit here?" Eve gestured to the chairs she assumed were for guests waiting to be seen. There sat an older woman who gave her a wide, friendly smile.

"Sure, dear. And don't let Thelma there bother you too much, okay?"

Eve nodded and sat down in the seat closest to the door. Thelma placed her bag on the seat between them and leaned over and said, "Ignore Rose. I promise I won't bother you." Eve's lips twitched and she sat back and watched as the scene in front of her played out.

"Stella, now you know I picked the bob first. You can't have it."

"Who says I can't, Sofia?"

"I said. You're always trying to take things I come up with first."

Sofia waved Stella off. "You're blowing things out of proportion and you know the hairstyle would look better on me."

Eve snorted. She could almost guarantee that these two

women were the twins that Kane had mentioned on the ride into town.

"Remember back in '64 when..."

Eve tuned out the argument. She was sure that anyone looking at her might think she was a little strange based on the amused expression on her face.

"So, when's the big day?"

Thelma's words caught Eve's attention, drawing her eyes away from the twins' bickering. "What do you mean 'big day'?"

"When are you and Kane going to get married?"

Eve was thankful that she hadn't been drinking anything at that moment because she knew it would have ended up down the front of her shirt. "We aren't?"

"I just assumed since you were living together—"

"Oh no, no. I'm staying with him temporarily while I sort some things out." She hoped that her overemphasis of the word *temporarily* would curb any other attempts or assumptions being made about the couple.

"Ah. Well, Stella and Sofia told me and Rose—"

Eve swung her head to look at Thelma. "This discussion was happening with Rose?"

Thelma nodded her head. Eve did everything in her power not to facepalm in real life.

"Based on what we've heard about you, dear, we think you two would be a perfect match."

"Ah. Okay? By the way, what have you heard about me?"

"Well, Rose told us that Kane had lovely things to say about you when he stopped by to check on Rose the other day." Thelma's wink told her that Eve that she knew exactly what she was doing by sharing this information.

"That's good, I guess."

"It is." Thelma leaned over and whispered, "And now Rose is probably going to try her utmost to make sure you get together." Her attention shifted just before her voice grew louder. "Rose, I ran into Abbie yesterday and she said she'd be in for a cut." Eve's ears perked up as she listened more closely at the mention of Abbie's name.

Rose nodded as Hensley appeared from the back and noticed that Eve was in the hair salon. "I'm so sorry that took so long."

"No worries." Lori walked out of the back as well and gave Eve smile and a wave before turning to talk to her mother.

"Are you ready to go?"

"Yep!" The two women waved goodbye to Rose, Lori, and the other patrons in the shop. It wasn't until she was seated in Hensley's car did she let out the breath she was holding in.

EVE OPENED the door and the first thing she noticed was that all the lights were off except for the television in Kane's living room.

She placed her bags near the stairs, intending to take them up with her later, and continued in to find Kane. He was sitting on the couch, enjoying what appeared to be an old football game; she was pretty sure football season was over.

"Hey."

Kane looked up and smiled at her before his eyes returned to the television. "Hey. Did you have fun with my sister?"

"I did, but I'm beat after she dragged me from store to store. Probably spent way too much money."

"Beat enough to not mind that I'm watching football right now and join me?"

Eve chuckled. "I'll have you know that I like football. I'm not a hardcore fan, but I've been to a few games."

"That's good to know."

"I'm going to grab a drink. Do you want anything?"

"Another beer if you don't mind."

Eve headed into the kitchen and opened the fridge. She smiled at the sight that greeted her. Kane had gotten her favorite soda, even though she told him not to. He must have remembered which soda she liked based on what he saw when he visited her apartment. She grabbed a soda and a beer and plopped down on the couch next to Kane.

"Thanks for grabbing my soda," she said as she handed him his beer.

"You're welcome."

"I'm probably making a bigger deal than there needs to be about this, but I truly appreciate it. Even down to the fact that you got the flavor I love."

Kane's eyes left the screen again, and he gave her a smile that almost set her ablaze. Although they were sitting in a dark room, she could see the smile had reached his eyes. "It wasn't any trouble at all."

She settled back in her seat and got comfortable.

"Maybe I was buttering you up, so you'd have no problem watching football tonight."

Eve slowly turned to him, and he couldn't keep his laughter to himself. "Just because I didn't want to watch the show you wanted to watch last night—"

"I'm kidding. Just trying to get a rise out of you and it worked. I apologize."

She thought about making a crack about how she could make something else rise but refrained. Plus, she was curious about who ended up winning this football game.

13

"Hey, this is last minute, but I'm going to take Ma and Grandma out for lunch. Do you want to go?"

Eve's head snapped up; she found Kane lounging on the doorjamb. The brown plaid shirt and dark-colored denim with the well-worn brown boots made him seem more relaxed and at home in Capitol versus the more professional attire she was used to seeing on him in in D.C.

"I need to wrap up this article and send it to my editor. I'll probably grab something quick from the kitchen." She was telling a white lie, but this was a great opportunity for her to snoop if she said so herself. The dejected look on his face, however brief, made her want to question him more, but she figured she could save that for later.

"How about we have them over for dinner in a couple of days? Maybe tomorrow or Friday?"

That was a great idea. She wished she could invite her girl-friends over, especially after their video chat, but she couldn't. Although she had nothing to complain about in staying with Kane, she did miss interacting with more people on a regular basis. She could tell when he registered her words because the creases in his forehead lifted and a small smile appeared on his face. "I'd like that."

Eve watched as he shifted his weight to stand and placed his hands in his pockets. "I'm going to head out now. Call or text if you need anything. I'll run those dates by 'em."

Eve smiled at his sudden slip into a more Southern accent. She wondered if he noticed that he did sometimes. "Sounds good. I'll see you later."

With that, she heard him walk down the steps and outside, the front door closing behind him. He had left the house. She waited a beat before she walked over to her bedroom window, overlooking the front yard, and she saw him close the door of the red pickup truck that he loved. He backed out of the driveway and jetted down the street.

Eve backed away from the window and headed down the stairs to the kitchen. She quickly scooped out some leftovers of the lasagna they had made the evening before, placed it into the microwave, and took a step toward the hallway. She hesitated for a moment, thinking she shouldn't be snooping, but he had given her access to his study... What was the harm in looking? She opened the door and it gave way a little too quickly. Eve grabbed the doorknob, careful not to let it bang against the wall. Thankfully, there was enough light in the space that she had no trouble locating the light switch that Kane had shown her during their tour. She stood there for a moment, second-guessing herself once again, before dragging her feet into the room.

Her first stop was Kane's desk. She eyed the papers that lie in a neat pile before fingering through them, trying her best not to disturb them too much. Nothing seemed weird or out of the ordinary. She hesitated. Should she open the desk drawers? Looking through something that was out in the open was one thing, but digging into someone's else drawers was a whole other thing, at least in her mind.

As she pulled her hand back, she accidentally hit the mouse. His computer screen to flicker on.

"Well, this qualifies as being out in the open," mumbled Eve as she scanned the contents on the screen. She was sure the gasp that fell from her lips could be heard from several counties over. On the screen were articles related to Representative Blake. "Why didn't he tell me he was digging into this case too?"

Her eyes scrolled across one window, eyeing the tabs that were open in the browser.

"'Blake tries to...' wait a minute." She clicked the tab and found an article she had written featuring quotes from Representative Blake. As Eve scrolled through the other tabs, she noticed he found several articles she had written, going back to the first few she ever published at the *Capitol Express*. "What do my older articles have to do with anything? Most of these aren't related to Blake at all." Why was he doing this?

Although she knew she shouldn't, curiosity got the best of her. Eve grabbed the mouse and closed one of the browser windows. Another gasp fell from her lips. Kane was digging into her past! There was information about the college she attended and some of her social media pages. There were also tabs open that contained information about Representative Blake as well. She found information about some of the bills he cosponsored, some of the events he attended and more. Was he trying to find a connection between them?

A slam of a car door in the distance stopped Eve's

thoughts from spiraling. She opened the window that she had closed on Kane's computer and took a giant step back before running up the stairs. She tried to stop her racing heart, but all thoughts of that were gone when she heard the doorbell sound throughout the house.

Her first instinct was to act like no one was home because that's what she would do if she was at her apartment during the day. But she wasn't at home, and everyone likely knew that Kane wasn't home based on how quick news traveled in this town. So, who was at the door?

Getting her food moved further down her list of priorities as she made her way to the front door. She peeped out one of the side windows and let out a sigh of relief when she saw Hensley standing on the porch. She unlocked the door, thankful that Kane was probably one of the few people in town to lock their door. Hensley greeted her with a bright smile.

"Hey! Just wanted to check in to see if you were settling in well."

"I am. Your brother went—"

"I know my brother is with my ma and grandma having lunch. I came by to check on you. I wanted to invite you to come hang with me and a few of my friends at Captain's Bar tonight. Figured it would be fun for you to let loose a bit. It also probably attracts the biggest crowds outside of the events Capitol throws together, like the spring fair."

Eve rolled the idea around in her mind. She missed her girlfriends at home, so maybe getting out would be beneficial.

"I'd love to join."

"Great! I'll pick you up around nine if that works for you?"

Eve nodded and waved before Hensley bounded down the steps and back to her car. Once she closed the door, her mind centered on finishing what she needed to do for work and picking out an outfit for the night; thoughts of what she had seen in the study moved to the back of her mind for the time being.

EVE WALKED out of the bathroom fanning herself. The instruments she used to style her hair caused a small sheen of sweat to break out across her skin. Part of her wished that she could tell Hensley that something came up and she couldn't make it. Then, she could throw on her sweatpants on just before curling up on the couch to watch a movie, but she knew she might regret it. Hanging out would be fun and would give her a bigger sense of what Capitol was about, so why shouldn't she go?

"Where are you going?"

Kane's voice startled her. There he was, leaning on the doorjamb once more. Eve wondered if that was his favorite spot in his home and if he would soon take up a permanent residence there.

"I'm going out with your sister and some of her friends. She stopped by today while you were at lunch with your mom and grandmother."

"Ah, Hensley said something about coming over here earlier. Are you gonna wear that?" he asked, and his tone made her glance over at him.

Why was he asking about what she was wearing? The black jeans she had on fit her like a second skin and the red short-sleeved top showed off her curves. The smokey-eye look and the darker red lipstick were also different from what she normally wore. She topped everything off with a black blazer and boots.

"Yeah. That was the plan."

"You look beautiful." He cleared his throat. "Well, I hope you have a good time tonight. And if you need anything, just text me. I'm happy to pick you up."

"Hensley offered to pick me up and drop me off so we should have it covered but thank you." Eve looked at him again and found him still inspecting her as his eyes traveled up and down her body—as if he were trying to commit her to memory. He didn't care that she could see him watching her. "Would you like to come?"

Kane shook his head. "No, I have some things I need to finish up here. Have a good time." He gave her a small smile and walked downstairs. Eve didn't realize she had been hoping that he would say yes until he walked away.

14

———

"What can I get y'all?"

The bartender's words brought Eve out of a daydream while she waited for Hensley to come back to the bar.

"Not sure what Hensley is having, but I'd like that IPA." Eve pointed to one of the beer dispensers.

"Oh, you must be Eve. Hensley mentioned that she was bringing you with her tonight. I'm Amber."

"Nice to meet you." The two women shook hands.

"I'll have that beer up for you in a second." Amber hurried away to get the drink, leaving Eve alone. Eve let her gaze float around the bar and compared Captain's Bar to the Green Hat. Where the Green Hat fully embraced an eighties and nineties vibe, Captain's Bar focused on a rustic feel. Woodsy decor mixed with low lighting, setting a comfortable mood. Eve could just make out that the bar's high-top tables were made out of wine barrels, which she thought added a cool touch to the space.

"Here you go." Amber set the drink in front of her. Eve took out some cash that she had brought with her.

"Nope! I thought I told you I was treating you tonight." Eve smiled at Hensley, who appeared over her shoulder. Hensley squeezed between Eve and another patron at the bar. "This is Mia."

"Nice to meet you."

"Likewise. Hensley here was telling us you needed an opportunity to have some fun."

"I guess I do. I didn't realize how much I needed it until she mentioned it, however. Writing and researching all of the time can and wear down anyone."

"Oh, what do you do?"

"I'm a journalist."

Mia perked up. "Oh really? I work for the *Independent Reporter*." She paused for a moment. "I'm not a journalist. I'm an admin."

It took everything in Eve to contain keep her mouth from swinging open. Had she really gotten this lucky? Before Eve could question her further, Mia flipped her long blonde hair over one shoulder and turned her attention back toward the bar. It was then that Eve realized that the ends of her hair were dyed pink. "You came to the right place and are hanging out with the right people." Mia whistled loudly, causing Eve and the patrons surrounding Mia to cover their ears. Eve glanced at Hensley, who had smartly plugged the ear closest to Mia. Hensley would be used to Mia's shenanigans. Amber, who had her back turned to the group near the beer taps, looked over and rolled her eyes.

"Mia, will you quit doing that? That is annoying as fuck."

At least she said it, Eve thought as she took another sip of her beer.

"When you hear that, you'll always know it's me."

"For better or for worse." Eve silently giggled at the words Hensley mumbled before Mia continued.

"I wanted to order shots of Fireball and whatever they wanted to drink."

Eve almost balked at the thought of taking a shot of Fireball but shrugged it off. This was supposed to be her opportunity to let loose. A shot of Fireball wouldn't kill her.

A couple of minutes later, Amber brought over three shots and placed one in front of each woman.

"Have fun, ladies." With that, Amber went back to her other customers.

"Who should we dedicate this to?" Mia picked up her shot and looked at the women.

"To new friends?" Eve asked, waiting to see if that was an acceptable thing to cheers to.

"To new friends!" Mia and Hensley said in unison as the three clinked their glasses together, brought the shots to their lips and downed the liquor.

"That. Was. A. Bit. Hot," Eve barely got out, shaking her head as the alcohol flowed through her body. "Or was it spicy? I'm not even sure."

Eve looked over and saw that Mia's eyes were closed. Before she could ask if everything was okay, Mia's eyes popped open, causing Eve to move her head back.

"That was ah-ma-zin!" Mia hooted and hollered and did a little jig. The excitement radiated off of her and Eve couldn't stop the grin from appearing on her face.

"Mia knows how to have a good time." Hensley's quiet

voice sounded in stark contrast to Mia's yelling. "But don't feel the need to keep up with her if you don't want to."

"I know, and that's cool." Eve cast a look over her shoulder and saw three men entered Captain's Bar. She thought nothing of it and let her eyes drift back to her new friends. She spared another glance at the front door and saw that one guy in the group had his eyes on Mia; he made his way over to them. Eve nudged Hensley and said, "Three men just entered and are headed our way."

Eve had hoped that Hensley would be discreet when she looked back, but quickly threw that thought out the window.

Hensley glared at the group before nudging Mia, who had since quieted down.

"Don't look now, Mia, but Connor and his friends are going to be here in a second."

Mia didn't bother turning around to confirm Hensley's statement. "I had a feeling he would show up."

The women weren't able to say anything else before Connor made his presence—and who he was there to see—known.

"Mia, I didn't expect to see you here."

Eve heard Hensley mumble something that sounded like *bullshit*. The three turned around to greet the new arrivals.

"Now, I thought we were going to keep this casual. I don't have to tell you where I'm going to be or who I'm going to be with."

Eve saw a change in his expression, but it lasted only a millisecond.

"I know, but that doesn't mean we can't hang out as friends."

Eve watched their body language as if she was interviewing a politician. She could tell that they liked each other, but something was keeping them apart. She made a note in her mind to ask Hensley on their drive home later.

Speaking of Hensley, Eve looked over to see what she had gotten herself into. Hensley was talking to one of the guys who had walked in with Connor as she was nursing a glass of water. Which potentially meant one thing.

"Hi."

Eve took a deep breath and maneuvered her body toward the speaker. She came face-to-face with a tall man—dirty blond hair and light eyes.

"Hey." She paused for a moment, debating what she should do about the situation. "I'm Eve."

"It's nice to meet you. I'm Trey."

"What he means is that he's James William III. But yes, his nickname is Trey."

"And you are?" Eve knew her tone was harsh, but she didn't like the interruption.

"Wyatt. I've known just about everyone here since we were in elementary school."

They were younger than Kane, being that Hensley was his baby sister. Trey shook his head. "Wyatt always gets a kick out of telling people my entire name." Wyatt clapped a hand over Trey's shoulder, and went back to his conversation with Hensley.

"Can I buy you another beer?"

Eve was somewhat shocked to find her glass almost empty; with all the excitement, she hardly remembered putting the glass up to her lips. "Uh, sure. I'll also take a water."

About ten minutes later, Eve found herself at a high-top

with the rest of the group. Mia and Wyatt traded insults; Hensley and Connor looked on laughing, while she and Trey talked quietly about how life differed in the nation's capital compared to life in Capitol, Virginia.

"I think I went to D.C. once or twice growing up."

Eve, who had taken another drink of water, stopped to swallow. "Oh really? Where did you go in the city?"

"I had to be an elementary school, and I think we visited one of the Smithsonians. I think it was the Air—" He paused. "I can't remember the name."

"The National Air and Space Museum?"

"That's it!"

The conversation with Trey was fine, but Eve knew it wasn't going anywhere. Trey was an attractive man, but the spark and the nervous excitement that she experienced in Kane's presence wasn't there. Even the dimple that appeared when he smiled wasn't enough to take her mind off of Kane. She kind of wished he had come out with them tonight.

"Trey, do you mind if I pull Eve away for a moment?" Hensley didn't wait for an answer before grabbing Eve's hand and leading her several feet away.

"What's up?"

"Kane just walked in." Speak of the devil.

"Wait, seriously? He said he didn't want to come."

"I'm usually able to read my brother pretty well, but I can't read the look on his face right now."

The look Kane served her could have melted steel. She was sure of it. The thought of what could be going through his mind both excited and frightened her. He would be standing in front of her in just a few quick seconds and she couldn't wait. Her wish that he had joined them on their evening out came to fruition, and it made her downright giddy.

"Hensley."

"Kane."

"Do you mind if I chat with Eve for a moment?"

Hensley took a small step back. "By all means, as long as you don't cause a scene."

That forced Kane to look at her. "When have I ever caused a scene?"

Eve saw Hensley open her mouth before snapping it shut again. She cast a look at Eve before walking away.

"I thought you didn't want to come out tonight?"

"I said I had some things to wrap up."

"I assume you finished those things?"

He took a step closer, his eyes fixated on her lips. "Your assumption would be correct." She took an involuntary step back and Kane took a step forward. Her body touched the wall behind her. She had nowhere to go unless through him, not that she wanted to go anywhere. That was a hard pill to swallow by itself.

Although he crowded her personal space, she didn't feel threatened. In fact, she felt safe. His body leaned into hers, and Eve held her breath. She knew the buzz in her mind was from one thing and it wasn't the beer. It was from being in his vicinity. Although they'd stood this close before, this time felt different. Much like the night they slept together all those years ago.

"I wanna leave."

"You want to go home?" His gaze slowly traveled up her face before meeting her eyes.

"Yeah. I think you and I have some things to talk about."

Without another word, Kane grabbed her hand and, with a quick wave to Hensley and her friends, he led her out of the bar. At his truck, he made sure she was comfortable in the passenger seat before walking around to the driver's side. A few ideas floated through her mind as she waited for him to enter the truck.

"Kane." Her voice came out raspier than she thought it would.

When he turned his head toward hers, the decision had been made. Her lips landed on his.

15

Eve could tell she shocked Kane when she kissed him. Hell, she shocked herself. But it didn't take him long to catch on and to catch up; he kissed her back with the same ferocity that she gave him. Although the center console was in the way, it did nothing to stop the intensity of their kiss. His hand drifted to her cheek, holding her as he tried to get even closer. Kane's other hand drifted down her body, scorching a path in its wake.

The sensations she was feeling brought only one question to the front of her mind: Why had she waited this long to kiss him again? But... now wasn't the time to think about the past or the time wasted. His hand that had made its home on her waist drifted back up her body and landed on her breast. He played with her nipple, making it grow taut before sliding his hand back down to her waist. She missed his touch on her nipple, but she wasn't about to stop to tell him so. Absentmindedly, she had placed her hand on his chest and it was heading south. Their kissing didn't stop, nor did they come up for air.

His kiss said so much, yet nothing at all. Had he wanted to kiss her for as long as she had wanted to kiss him? Did his thoughts veer to her as much as hers did to him? His tongue struck the right chords in her mouth as the two dueled for control of the kiss. The nerves and excitement she felt in his presence increased tenfold as Eve allowed her hand to move freely across his chest. Her hand splayed across his pec, and she could feel the beating of his heart. It wasn't long before her hand glided down his chest and across his abs. She took her time to feel each and every stretch of defined muscle. Her hand made its way down to his crotch and he gasped. Kane wasn't expecting that. He grew even harder under her hand and broke their kiss.

"Is this how you want this to go, sweetheart?" He asked, his voice thick with arousal making his Southern accent even more pronounced. Eve was momentarily taken aback by the endearment. Normally the term would have pissed her off, given how many times a man had called her that when they were trying to be condescending about something, mostly at work. But when it came from his lips... she nearly flew off the seat and into his lap. *If only the console wasn't in the way.*

"What do you think?" She asked pointedly placing small kisses on his lips. That lasted only a moment before his hands clasped her cheeks and his lips were once again on hers for another long, sensual kiss.

A knock on the driver's-side window startled the couple apart. They swung around to look at the disrupter, and Kane sighed loudly when he realized who it was.

"Axel, don't you have something else to do? Anything?"

Axel chuckled. "I have plenty to do but was curious to see what was up when I saw you hop in the car, but you didn't pull out." He paused for a moment. "I guess that could be taken several ways."

Eve giggled while Kane let out a growl. "Everything is fine, as you can see."

"Yes, it is. I'm messing with you, man. I'll let you two get on your way."

"Thanks, and don't tell Ma."

"Since I was checking on you under the guise of official police business, I won't. But if someone else saw you two, there isn't anything I can do about that."

Kane nodded and Eve gave Axel a small wave as he left the couple alone once more.

Neither of them said a word as they buckled their seat belts and Kane drove them home. Eve was worried about breaking the silence, but the quiet bothered her. She could feel the nervous energy bouncing around the car, but she didn't know if it only came from her. Eve looked at Kane out of the side of eye and found him staring ahead at the road in front of him.

When they arrived back at Kane's, he opened the door without using a key and Eve said, "Couldn't get away with that in D.C."

"The joys of small-town living," he replied as he closed the door. Quietness passed between them. Eve didn't know if she should even try to keep the conversation going. The adrenaline that she had experienced from kissing Kane in public to getting caught by Axel was waning.

"So, you think Axel will actually keep quiet about what he saw? You told me about how news spreads in this town."

"As far as he's concerned, nothing happened."

"Do you want to pretend too? That nothing happened?"

The words came out more sheepish that Eve was hoping, but they were out there.

His usually light hazel eyes took on a darker tinge. She might have gone a step too far.

"Do you remember the night that we slept together?"

How could she forget? She made a noncommittal noise, not saying yes but not saying no.

"I think you remember that day like it was yesterday. Just like I do. Do you want to know what else I'm thinking?"

"Yes," Eve said, although she worried about what he might say.

"I wish that you had worn a dress tonight because it would have made it easier to fuck you."

If she hadn't been turned on from their kissing in the car, she was now. He stepped forward and gave her a kiss, more sensual than the one in the car. It was slow and his hands stayed on her face this time. His actions were more controlled, like a trapeze artist walking a tightrope. His words floated in her head as she imagined what it would be like if he fucked her.

She stepped back and took a deep breath. "There is one thing I wanted to know."

"Yes?"

"Did you decide to come to Captain's because you finished whatever it was you were working on, or was it because you were worried I'd go home with someone else?" That was a mouthful, Eve thought as she waited for his response.

The smirk she had grown to like reappeared on his face. "What do you think?"

His question took Eve by surprise, leaving her

temporarily speechless. She hoped it was a mixture of both; she leaned more toward the latter, but she didn't want to utter those words out loud.

"That you wanted it to be known I was with you and only you."

"Ding, ding, ding." The smirk deepened before he said, "Good night."

"Good night to you too," Eve said as she watched Kane walk up the stairs. She went into the kitchen and grabbed a glass of water. After taking a few sips, she too walked up the stairs and closed her door behind her. She placed the glass of water on her bedside table and turned around to walk toward the bathroom. Before she could take a step, her eyes were drawn to the crack underneath her door and she watched as the light in his bedroom flicked on briefly before turning off. With that, she headed into the bathroom and took her time removing the makeup, washing her face, and brushing her teeth. She turned the light off and headed back into her room. Eve was soon in bed, staring up at the ceiling, wondering about what had transpired that night and how it would affect their relationship. She fell into a restless sleep.

Eve wrapped up the article she was working on for Casey and checked the time. It was just after 3:00 p.m., giving Eve plenty of time to do some more research into the hit and run. Earlier that morning, Eve checked Capitol's newspaper, the *Independent Reporter*, but couldn't find anything referencing the incident. She needed to find another avenue to gather information pertaining to the accident. Capitol didn't allow the public to review police reports because the Virginia Freedom of Information Act usually kept the report confidential. She sat back to think about her next move and an idea popped into her head.

She packed her laptop and a few other essentials into her book bag. She threw on the denim jacket she had tossed on her bed earlier that day and grabbed her bag before heading downstairs. She found Kane sitting at the dining room table with his laptop open, talking to someone on his cell phone. It shocked Eve that he hadn't gone down to his study to work, but maybe he needed a change of scenery. When she stepped on a creaky floorboard, he looked up and mouthed the words, "one second." She didn't have much of a choice because, in order to make this work, she needed something from him.

"What's up?" he asked once he got off the phone.

"Can I borrow your SUV?" She could sense his hesitation. "I swear I have a clean driving record."

Kane stood up and walked into the kitchen. He came back with a pair of car keys. "Be careful with my baby."

Eve rolled her eyes and laughed. "I promise I'll be careful." She walked toward the front of the house and yelled over her shoulder, "I'm sure you'll have fun readjusting the seat and mirrors when you get back in it."

Eve chuckled at Kane's groan, but stopped when he called her name.

"Don't forget Ma and Grandma are coming over this evening." Eve turned around and looked at him. "You forgot, huh?" It was his turn to laugh at her.

"Shit. I guess I did. I forgot we agreed to today and not Friday. Do you have any plans for what you want to cook? I think I promised to cook and—"

"Don't worry about it. How about you text me what you want me to pick up and I'll start on it if you aren't back in a couple of hours?"

Eve smiled at their teamwork. "Thank you. I'm headed to the library."

"You're welcome." Kane walked over to her and gave her a kiss on the lips. His actions took her by surprise. "That's payback for the one you threw at me last night."

"Well, clearly you enjoyed it."

"I did."

Eve hadn't expected him to be so upfront with his answer. "You know we need to talk about all of that anyway."

"I know, but we can save it for later unless you don't want to head to the library?"

Eve glanced at the front door before looking back at Kane. "I should probably get to the library and do what I need to do there before your mom and grandma come by." Putting a bit of distance between them might do them some good.

Kane nodded. "Just let me know about dinner."

And, with that, she closed the door.

ALTHOUGH IT TOOK her some time to adjust the SUV to her liking, Eve made it to the library with no trouble. She shut off the GPS on her phone before placing it in her pocket and grabbing her book bag from the passenger seat. She locked the car doors and headed toward the library. She sent Kane a quick text message about throwing together shrimp scampi with a fresh salad for dinner before pulling open the front door and entering the library.

The library was one story but filled to the brim with books of all different genres. Close to the front desk she could see a section marked off for children that contained a small play area. With a quick smile and wave to the librarian, Eve set up at an unoccupied table. Her primary aim for this visit was to find out more information about that hit and run that happened fifteen to twenty years ago. She hoped that, somewhere in the library, there might be some record of which articles ran during those years.

The thing that was time-consuming was her not knowing

when the incident occurred, but maybe doing a search under the victim's name might help? Eve realized that Kane hadn't given her Abbie's full name, making the search more difficult, but she was determined not ask more questions, in case it made him more suspicious. She had to take matters into her own hands.

She searched for "Abby" and "hit and run" on the *Independent Reporter*, but found nothing. Eve growled under her breath in frustration. Was there no record of the accident at all? That would be too strange, but maybe it meant that she was on the right track. Was someone was trying to hide the fact that this incident occurred. Then another idea popped into her head.

What if she was spelling her name incorrectly? She then typed in "Abbie" and scanned the articles that popped up.

"Bam," she said as she found an article that looked promising. The article talked about how Abbie Henderson was still in the hospital, but she was doing well and would be released shortly. Although the article glazed over details of the accident, it provided a date and gave her the victim's full name.

Eve searched again— "Abbie Henderson"—and found articles that painted the picture of someone who was well regarded in her community and records of the various awards she won throughout her school career. But things became quiet around the time she was released from the hospital. Eve needed more information.

Eve stood up from the table and headed back to the front desk.

"Excuse me?" she asked the librarian. The older woman turned around and greeted her with a smile.

"How can I help you?"

"Um, I was looking to see if you had any clips or slides, or maybe a database of older articles from the *Independent Reporter*?"

The librarian's face lit up. "Yes, we do! Wait one second." She bent down and pulled out a piece of paper. "One database that you can access only from the library includes articles that published in the *Independent Reporter*. This piece of paper can help you access the database from your own laptop or from the library's."

Eve thought she might have just gotten lucky. "Would you say that this database has more information or articles than the one that is currently on the newspaper's website?"

The librarian nodded her head. "If you're looking for something in particular and can't find it, I'll be shocked. But if you're having any trouble, let me know and I'll do my best to help."

Her words and easygoing nature made Eve smile. "Okay, I'll let you know if I have any other questions. Thank you so much."

"No problem, ma'am."

With that, Eve went back to her table and soon she was staring at the database. She checked that her search would be for articles from the *Independent Reporter* and, taking a deep breath, she typed in Abbie Henderson's name. Eve scanned the results and gasped. "Woman Victim of Hit and Run. Suspect at Large."

Eve scanned the article and realized that it had been published on the front page of the *Independent Reporter*. So why did she have trouble finding it on the *Independent Reporter*'s website when it was easy to find through the library database? She made a note to contact Hensley to find out if she could ask Mia a quick question. Suddenly, dread coursed through her veins. Was someone trying to hide the fact that this accident occurred in Capitol?

"DINNER WAS DELICIOUS. THANK YOU BOTH." Lori beamed at her son and Eve as she rested a hand on her belly.

Eve smiled back as Kane gestured to her plate. She nodded and he grabbed her plate before heading over to his grandma.

"You both put together a splendid meal. You and my grandson here make a wonderful team." Rose winked before patting Eve on the hand as Kane brought the dishes in the kitchen.

Eve almost wanted to bet that Kane had rolled his eyes. "Grandma, stop it."

"What? I'm just saying you should take Eve out on a date instead of keeping her cooped up in this house."

Eve chuckled. "Dinner was mostly Kane's doing. I was at the library doing some research."

"What were you researching?"

Eve debated her answer as she recalled Kane saying how quickly word spread in this town. She didn't want to let it be known she was even remotely considering that Representative Blake might be tied to Abbie's accident. But it wouldn't hurt to have input from someone who was there and might remember what happened at the time.

"I was doing some research on Capitol and realized that

there was a hit-and-run accident that happened about eigh-teen years ago?"

Rose's expression went from relaxed to worried in two seconds flat. "You're talking about what happened with Abbie."

Eve nodded as Kane entered the room. "What are you all talking about?"

"Abbie Henderson," Lori said. Kane raised an eyebrow at Eve but said nothing.

"Kane, I'm not sure how much you remember."

"I remember all the hoopla surrounding it, but not much else. I kept my head down and focused on trying to get through school to join the Marines."

Rose nodded. "What I remember is she was back from college for the summer and she worked at Capitol Diner to earn some money for the next school year." Lori nodded along. "Her car was in the shop, but she didn't live too far from the diner, so she walked home. And one evening a car hit her. I believe she had a broken arm and leg and a few other injuries. The driver fled the scene and was never charged. Although the circumstances of her accident were horrible, the community really came together to support her."

"Does Abbie still live in the area?"

Lori nodded. "She lives next door to her parents, who still live near the diner." It took everything for Eve to not jump for joy. She wanted to figure out how she could talk to her—if Abbie would be up for it.

Eve, Kane, Lori, and Rose continued talking for a while before Lori declared that the two of them needed to head home. After some quick goodbyes, Eve and Kane were alone once more.

"Well, that went better than I thought it would." Eve stretched after Kane closed the door, locking the rest of the world out.

"It did. And I want to take some of my grandmother's advice."

"What's that?"

"I want to take you out on a date."

17

———

Eve twisted her body to get a better look at the pale-yellow dress she had put on. *Not too bad*, she thought as she twirled around once more. She was thankful for the warmer weather as the winter slowly moved into spring. With a thick denim jacket and brown ankle boots, she was ready to go.

She saw out of the corner of her eye when Kane appeared at her door and glanced into the room. That glance wasn't enough because he did a double take. With a second look, his gaze scorched a path down her body and back up again. It took everything in her to control the shiver that threatened to leave her body. How could she be turned on just by someone studying her body? She wanted to tell him to forget going out on the date but her thoughts were interrupted. Her phone vibrated on the desk, breaking up the moment they shared. She snatched it and looked at the screen, finding a text message from an unknown number.

Unknown Number: *Hey, Eve, this is Mia. Hensley told me that you wanted to get in touch with me?*

Eve recalled sending Hensley a message last night. Hensley promised to let Mia know that Eve wanted to get in touch with her.

Eve: Hi Mia! I want to let you know that I had a great time hanging out with you at Captain's Bar the other night. I also had a quick question related to the Independent Reporter, *but I wasn't sure if you had the answer.*

Mia: I had a great time meeting you as well! Go for it. What's your question?

Eve: Is there a reason that an article wouldn't appear on the Independent Reporter's *website but would appear in the library's database? I was doing some research into the history of Capitol. I found some articles appeared through the library's search engine, but I couldn't find those same articles on the* Independent Reporter's *site.*

Mia: Huh. That's interesting. I know we rebuilt our website from the ground up about six months ago so maybe some of the articles that you found on the library website didn't make it over to the new website?

Eve could see how that might have happened, but if a story made the front page... You'd think that whomever did the migrating would make sure that those stories were put up first, no matter how long ago the article was written and published.

Mia: On the other hand, maybe there was some sort of bug and some articles were missed? I can see if the company we used can go back and double check.

Mia's explanation seemed plausible, but Eve couldn't stop the thoughts running through her head. If this was such a big story when it happened, why would it not be included in the website's archives?

"You ready?" The words tumbled off his lips and made her body temperature rise a few degrees, much like that first sip of whiskey. Kane's tight, long-sleeved brown shirt hugged his muscles, making Eve yearn to be pulled into his solid chest. The dark colored jeans fit his legs perfectly and visions of what Kane might look like without them crossed her mind. She lightly shook her head, keeping those thoughts at bay.

"I think so," she said as she ran a hand through her hair one more time before grabbing her purse and placing her phone in it. It felt good to leave her book bag behind for just one night. No worries about Representative Blake. No worries about work. No worries about the fact that she was miles away from her home. Tonight was about her and Kane.

"Where are we going?" she asked once Kane pulled out of the driveway and hit the road.

"We're gonna go to this fancy restaurant in the next town over," he said as the truck hummed down the street.

"Sounds great." She pressed the button to roll down the window, letting the cool breeze flow between the couple. The sun was setting, reminding her of the sunrise as they fled DC. Feelings of home and missing her life there circled around her—causing sadness that she had done so well to keep at bay until now. She fought off the tears and pulled herself together without drawing a reaction from Kane. Eve was happy about that because she didn't want to explain to him how she felt if she could avoid it.

It didn't take long for a couple to arrive at Cuisine Grove. The atmosphere differed completely from the one she was growing accustomed to at Capitol Diner. Without a doubt, aesthetically speaking, this place was fancier, but that didn't mean the food was as good as the food at the diner.

Kane leaned over from across the table. "Now, I will admit that this food is tasty, but it's not as tasty as my mom's."

This statement made Eve chuckle, especially since he had just read her mind.

"Good to know," she said, and she turned her attention to the menu.

Once they placed their orders, Eve leaned back and took a sip from her wine, opting for that over beer. "I don't know if I've ever told you, but I wanted to say thank you."

"Thank you for what?" The Southern drawl shined tonight, making her a lucky woman.

"Thank you for allowing me to stay here with you for a bit. Thanks for introducing me to your hometown. People are so friendly. It must have been a great place to grow up."

Kane waited a moment before commenting. "Every place has its difficulties, but I don't regret growing up in Capitol. By the way, I'd totally recommend the filet mignon. They make a mean steak here."

"But not as tasty as your mom's." Kane laughed after Eve threw his words back at him. "I'm glad that you like Capitol since you want to move back. Your love for your hometown runs deep."

"Speaking of my hometown, it seems to love you back. I swear, the number of texts I get from my sister alone is enough to show how popular you are here."

Eve laughed before taking another sip of her wine. "Hensley is fantastic, and it's been nice having someone to hang out with, especially since I'm missing my girls at home."

Kane's face took a dramatic turn and looked taken aback. "And what am I, chopped liver?" The smile that appeared on his face told her he was kidding.

Eve cracked up. "You know you're not. I think I proved that the night you dropped into Captain's Bar." She crossed her arms over her chest and raised an eyebrow. Eve watched as Kane's eyes briefly dipped down to her breasts and back up to her face. She hadn't done it to get that reaction, but she wasn't mad either.

"So, you mean to tell me you didn't have another agenda when you came into Captain's Bar?"

"As we hear a lot in D.C., I plead the fifth." Kane brought the gin and tonic he was drinking up to his lips. Eve snorted, trying to contain the giggles that threatened to escape.

"Come on, you can admit it. We are in a secluded part of a very romantic restaurant. Lay it on me."

"I don't think we have the same thing in mind in terms of me laying something on you."

Eve grinned before biting her lip. "You remember when you asked me a few nights ago if I remembered the night we spent together?"

Kane nodded but said nothing, so Eve continued by whispering, "I remember it vividly. In fact, I replay certain scenes while I'm alone and I—"

Kane's groan stopped her in her tracks. "I'd love to continue this conversation after we finish dinner and can get out of here."

Eve sat back with a satisfied smirk. "You started it."

"I know and I regret it—for now."

"Just now?"

"I think the tables will be turned by the end of the night."

18

———

"Cuisine Grove is a great restaurant," Eve said as she placed her purse on the couch. She took off her jacket and threw it over her arm. "Thanks for taking me."

"It was my pleasure. There's one thing that's missing."

"What's that?"

"A good-night kiss."

Eve looked down at her feet and smiled before looking back up at Kane. "Sounds like you need to walk me to my room."

Kane chuckled. "That could be arranged." He gestured toward the stairs. "After you."

Eve smiled, grabbed her purse, and the duo climbed up the stairs. As they reached her room, Eve said, "So, this is it."

"It doesn't have to be."

Kane didn't give Eve a chance to respond before he closed the gap between them and his lips met hers. His mouth covered up her groan. The taste of gin was still on his lips as Kane maneuvered them around and started backing her into another doorway. It didn't take long for her to realize he had redirected her into his bedroom.

Eve broke the kiss. "Guess what?"

Kane regarded her with a raised eyebrow. "What?"

"I'm wearing a dress today."

Those words were all it took before he was back on her. His hands cupped her face as he tried to deepen the kiss, but they didn't stay there long.

They moved down her neck toward her breasts. He played with them through her dress. She could feel her hardened nipples brushing up against her bra. He returned his hands to her shoulders, walked her to the bed, and, with a gentle push, she was flat on her back.

She looked up at him and the hands that had tortured her framed her head, him enclosing her in his orbit. He crept down her body and stopped once his hands reached her thighs.

"You mentioned that you were wearing a dress tonight. Is that right?"

"Yes," she whispered. She felt his fingertips lightly caress her thighs and she shivered at the touch.

"Well, we can't have that go to waste, can we?"

His eyes stayed on her as he bunched up the dress, moving it out of his way. He spread her legs wide, giving himself more to work with. His fingers gently touched her through her panties, and she almost bucked off the bed. What would it be like when he touched her once she was bare? She didn't have long to wait because Kane pushed her panties to the side.

"You know what we didn't do when we fucked all those

years ago?" His eyes moved from her mound up to her eyes. "I don't think that will be an issue tonight."

The noise that left Eve's mouth wasn't human, she was sure of it. Kane had her open to the world and at his mercy as he alternated his motions—giving her an immense amount of pleasure. She could feel the pressure building up inside her and it wasn't long before she came. Her thighs launched off the bed. "Kane! Oh, my—"

He slowed his movements down as she came down off her high. He threw her a cocky grin as he whipped his shirt over his head. Speaking of cocky... Kane's hands went to his jeans and took them off within seconds. In just his boxers, he walked over to the bedside table and picked up a condom. She watched as he rolled the condom on his dick and he looked over at her. "Close your eyes."

His request took Eve by surprise, but she did it anyway.

She couldn't hear much, but what she felt made her want to buck again. He crawled back onto the bed and she could feel him positioning himself between her legs. Kane ran his cock up and down her opening, making her want to pull him into her herself.

He eased himself into her and she moaned, enjoying the sensations he was giving to her. He did a few small pumps before going in deeper.

"Are you ready?"

"Been ready."

Next thing she knew, his hands were on her waist and his dick was buried completely in her.

The gentleness he started off with was nowhere near the pace he kept now. His thrusts made her want to scream out in pleasure.

As if he could hear her thoughts, he said, "I can tell you want to yell. Don't worry, the neighbors can't hear you."

Eve's laugh turned into a gasp as he continued fucking her. She was right. There was no one nearby who could hear her. She could feel her body about to reach the edge and he knew she was close too.

"Come," was all he said before she went off the cliff that Kane had figuratively placed her on. He soon followed her with a groan. He lay on her for a moment, trying to catch his breath.

"Why did we wait this long to have sex again?"

Kane chuckled. "Because it pissed you off that I left before you woke up the next morning."

"Yeah, that was pretty messed up."

"I got called away and had to deal with something." He sighed and ran a hand through his hair. "I'm sorry once again. I should have said something."

"Eh. I'm over it. And don't want to think about it anymore because it will put a damper on the sex we just had."

"That's true," he said as he pulled out of her. Eve watched him as he walked toward his bathroom. Then she threw her body back on the bed.

"WELL, this is not something I'm used to."

"What's that?"

"Falling asleep next to someone."

Eve agreed with him but said nothing. After all, it was still the night of their first proper date.

"I rarely sleep with men on the first date."

Kane let out a belly laugh. "That was random. Although that was technically our first date, I think we are past that point. Hell, technically we're living together."

"Eh, kind of?" She wanted to give him a bit of a hard time to see where he was going with this.

"Well, we take turns cooking dinner and doing dishes. We've gone grocery shopping together, have hung out with my family, separately and together I might add. We've even argued over what television show to watch."

"So, what you're saying is that we've been unofficially together since we got here."

"Pretty much."

Neither one of them said anything, not wanting to acknowledge the elephant in the room.

"Are you busy tomorrow?"

Eve was glad Kane broke the stalemate. "I don't think so. What's up?"

"Hensley wants me to look at some things at her bakery tomorrow and I thought maybe you would want to come? It shouldn't take long."

Eve remembered the last time a Slade told her that something wouldn't take long and snickered to herself.

"What's so funny?"

Eve shook her head. "Nothing. Sure, I'd love to see Hensley's shop."

"Would you want to stop by the fair after that?"

"Hmm? What fair?" She paused for a hot second and as Kane opened his mouth to reply, she continued, "Is this the spring fair? I think Hensley mentioned it."

Kane nodded. "I'm not sure how much she told you, but every year, Capitol puts together a fair in the spring to celebrate our town's founding. I figure we can head over there this evening."

"I'd love to."

"And then next weekend, Capitol Diner is hosting a food drive for the homeless in the county. Thought you might want to go to that."

Eve nodded against Kane's chest. "Sounds like our social calendar is filling up."

"That it is."

A noise from the floor made Eve jump.

"What the heck was that?"

Kane moved his arm from around her and sat up. "I think it might have been my phone vibrating," he said as he got up out of the bed.

Eve took her time ogling him in all his naked glory. The light from the lamp on his bedside table bathed Kane in a warm glow. He walked over to the foot of the bed and picked up the jeans he had been wearing earlier that night. He rifled through his pants pocket and pulled out his phone. His expression didn't change as he viewed what Eve assumed was a message.

"Is everything all right?" Eve asked

"Yeah. I have to head downstairs for a bit and work on this, but it shouldn't take too long."

Eve knew it had to be past 10:00, so the chances of this having to do with the foundation were slim in her mind. "Okay, I guess I can go back to my room." She started getting up and pulled a sheet to her chest.

"No. You can stay here if you want. It shouldn't take too long. Plus, we should be ready for round three by the time I return." His smoldering gaze and the smirk he sent made her quiver. He left her stunned and no words left her mouth. "I'll see you soon."

Kane put on his boxers and jeans before walking over to her. He laid a kiss on her lips and on her forehead before he left the room.

She grabbed the remote from his bedside table. It took a couple of tries to figure out how to turn it on. But, after flipping through the channels, she concluded that there was nothing on television. She flipped through the channels again and landed on the local news. Placing the remote next to her on the bed, she stood up and found the shirt that Kane had worn earlier that night. She put it on and she climbed back in the bed to take a better look around his room, as she had been preoccupied earlier.

The bedroom looked like the stereotypical bachelor pad, with dark colors everywhere—including the wood that made up his bedroom set, the sheets on the bed, and the big screen television that hung on the wall opposite. She leaned over to Kane's side of the bed and turned off the lamp. Wait, since when did Kane have a specific side of the bed? This was his bed, in his room, in his house. Eve's thoughts stopped in their tracks when the news broadcast on the screen distracted her.

"In other news, Capitol's own Representative Anthony Blake, a rising star in Congress, will attend Capitol's annual Founder's Day Fair tomorrow. He and his father, Capitol Mayor Jeff Blake, are expected to make speeches at the event."

Representative Blake was going to be back in the area? She stumbled out of Kane's bed and looked around. Where the hell had her purse landed? She found her dress on the floor and picked it up.

"Ah, there you are," she muttered.

Eve picked up her purse and pulled her phone out. A few swipes confirmed that the House of Representatives was on a recess, which meant that a lot of the congressional members would head back home to meet with constituents and hold events in the district. Although there was no timeline for her to uncover his secret, she felt a renewed sense of pressure to figure out if Representative Blake was connected to Abbie's accident. Especially if it meant doing it before whoever was trying to hurt her could find her in Capitol.

19

———

Eve felt soft kisses, nips, and licks on her back, but the desire to wake up wasn't there. Waking up would have taken more strength than she was willing to give.

"What are you doing?" Her voice was muffled under a pillow.

"Trying to wake you up. Is it working?"

A smile crept across Eve's face, although he couldn't see it. She lifted her head with her eyes still closed and said, "No. I had a long night." Then she let her head flop back onto the pillow.

Kane chuckled. "We need to get ready to head to Hensley's."

"Oh, that's right." But Eve didn't move.

"Could I entice you by saying that Hensley has some of the most amazing cookies in the world?"

Eve opened her eyes. "I'm always in the mood for cookies."

"Then let's go," Kane said as he patted her on the butt before climbing out of bed.

ONCE THEY LEFT Kane's house, it didn't take long for the couple to reach Hensley's bakery. Sweet Treats sat on a street with endless shops and a couple of eateries. It was where Hensley had taken Eve to go shopping a while back, but Eve didn't remember getting a glimpse of it. Pink decorations adorned the storefront, surrounding its name, and included a cupcake painted on the glass storefront. Eve thought the branding was adorable.

Kane opened the door and a tiny bell rang. The first thing that Eve noticed was the smells that caressed her like a quiet, cozy evening at home. If the decor of this place didn't tell you it was a bakery, the smell of baked goods and desserts did.

"This bakery is adorable," she said as she looked around. The branding on the outside of the shop meshed well with the brightly colored decor on the inside. A mural on one wall included many desserts such as cake, brownies, doughnuts, and pies, but was created in such a way that it looked fun and classy.

"It's very interesting that all the women in your family went into small businesses, Kane."

He paused and looked at Eve as he thought about her comment. "You know I never really thought about that, but yeah, the entrepreneurial spirit seems to run deep in my grandma, mom, and sister. They truly excel in them. I know that they could be probably doing a million different other things, but this makes them happy." After he said that, Hensley appeared from the back.

"Hey! Thanks for coming over. Kane, I wanted you to look at the security cameras we just installed."

That news shocked Eve. As far as she could see, Capitol was relatively quiet with no crime to speak of. Kane had left the front door to his house unlocked several times, something she never would have thought to do in D.C. Although it never hurt to have more security, the decision to do so was interesting to Eve and sent her curiosity through the roof. "Why are you installing security cameras? Did something happen?"

Hensley shifted on her feet. She looked at Kane and then back at Eve before answering. "It's nothing too bad, but we've had someone breaking into cars on this strip recently. I was hoping to be vigilant about catching whoever it was. I'm not talking about breaking in as in someone breaking the window of the car. More along the lines of folks here never had a reason to lock their cars, so we don't, and now someone is rifling through people's things. Taking odds and ends. Axel and Kane both thought it was a good idea, so here we are."

Eve nodded her head, understanding where Hensley was coming from. Kane waved before walking into what Eve assumed was a back room where the security feed was set up. Eve sat down at a table in the shop.

"Anyway, would you like something to eat while Kane examines this? I'm hoping that he can streamline the setup so it's easier for everyone to use."

"I'd love something. How about a croissant?"

"I'll bring that right out for you." Hensley grabbed the treat, placed it on a plate and walked over to Eve.

"How many people work here?"

"We have two full-time employees and Esther works here part time. She said getting up and coming here help keeps her active and she's been fantastic, so it works out great for all of us. Here you go." Hensley handed Eve the croissant and sat down in the seat opposite her.

Eve debated her what she should say. She wanted to ask about how to get in contact with Abbie and what they knew about the accident, but she knew she risked someone putting the pieces together as to why she had come to Capitol. Well, one reason why she had come to Capitol. Eve thought if she said it in the right way, she wouldn't draw attention to herself.

"Is it all right if I ask you something?" Eve asked.

Hensley raised a skeptical eyebrow at her. "Sure. Ask me anything."

"So, I was in the library the other day doing some research on Capitol. I found out about this horrible accident that happened to a woman named Abbie Henderson years ago." There, she thought to herself. Hopefully, that wouldn't be too attention grabbing.

"Yeah, I think I was in middle school at that time because Kane and Axel were in high school. Anyway, from what I remember, and what I was told, it was horrific what happened to her. In fact, the person still hasn't been brought to justice." Hensley had a faraway look in her eyes. "I think it has somewhat been a black spot in town."

"Really?" asked Eve. "How so?"

"There's been this kind of weird energy that appears whenever someone brings it up, at least in my presence. I mean, most of the people who live here either remember it happening or were told about it to remind people that they need to be careful, especially when walking alone at night. I think most of Capitol's residents believe that someone who wasn't from around here committed the hit and run. So, the risk of this potentially happening again is less likely, if that makes sense."

Eve debated how to ask her next question, given the information that Hensley had just shared with her. "I think I saw that Abbie still lives nearby."

Hensley nodded her head. "She does. She's married now and has two children of her own. I run into her quite a bit."

"Why is that?"

"She has a small business, too, and we both usually have booths at the farmers' market."

A light bulb went off in Eve's head. "So, would an event like tonight's Founder's Day Fair potentially have a farmers' market?"

Hensley leaned back in her chair. "Actually, yes it does. I'll be there, and I assume Abbie will be too."

Eve took a bite of the croissant and chewed, buying herself time to think of something else to say. "Oh great, Kane and I were planning on attending tonight. So, I guess we'll see you there."

"That you will," Hensley said just before the door chime rang. "I need to go help a customer, but I'll see you soon."

"Sounds good," Eve said as she went back to the delicious croissant. She couldn't wait to go to the fair tonight since it meant that all the people who played a starring role in this enormous secret might be in the same place at the same time.

～

EVE AND KANE spent most of the day relaxing around his home until it was time to leave for the fair.

Eve threw together an outfit that consisted of jeans, a dark purple shirt, her ankle boots, and a blazer to go with Kane's blue-and-white-plaid shirt, jeans, and boots. The Founder's Day Fair was being held at a vast lot about fifteen minutes outside the center of town. By the time they arrived, the fair was in full swing, but Eve knew that Representative Blake wasn't supposed to speak for another hour. Eve and Kane browsed the many shops and booths at the farmers' market, noting things they might want to buy. It wasn't long before they found Hensley with a huge line surrounding her booth.

"You think we can help her?" Eve asked.

"I don't know if there are certain protocols that need to be in place in order for us to be behind the table."

"But it would only be for a few minutes, I assume."

Kane nodded. "Let's head over there and see what we can do to help her and the staff get the number of customers under control." The duo walked over to the Sweet Treats booth, and when Hensley looked up at them, Eve could see her visible sigh of relief.

"If you guys don't mind, could you take ringing people up? The prices per item should already be listed on the iPad." They nodded their heads and walked around the back of the booth. It wasn't long before the line for Sweet Treats was under control.

Once that happened, Hensley pulled Kane and Eve aside and said, "Okay, you guys are now off the hook." She wiped her arm across her forehead. "Thanks for everything."

"No worries. We are happy to help."

"Speak for yourself." Kane's words earned him two

elbows to the gut. One of the other staffers asked for Kane's help to unload a few things, so off he went. Eve chuckled to herself, looked across the way, and noticed several of the other booths in the vicinity. "Oh, I want to go check out that booth right there. It looks like they're selling bath and beauty products."

Hensley looked up and said, "Oh yeah, I love their stuff. You should go over there." She then leaned over and whispered in Eve's ear, "Abbie owns that business."

Eve didn't react to her words outwardly, but on the inside, her heart was thumping as if she had just run a half-marathon. She didn't want to alert anyone around her that the news had turned her mind upside down. She might have found a way to talk to Abbie without having to come up with an excuse. Seeing that Kane was still busy moving things, Eve excused herself and maneuvered her way through the crowd to reach Bluebird Beauty.

A woman with her long red hair in a messy bun turned to Eve, a smile on her face. "Hi, my name is Abbie. Can I help you with anything?"

"I'm Eve and it's nice to meet you. I was hoping to pick up some bath bombs for myself and my friends back home."

"Well, you've come to the right place. Here are the ones we have in stock. Let me know if you have questions or if you want to know about any of the products we have displayed here or in our booth."

"Thanks, will do." Eve sat back on her heels before looking down to get a good look at the display. But her mind was elsewhere; she needed to talk to Abbie about the accident, if she was up for it. After selecting several bath bombs,

Eve picked up a few lip balms and herbal soaps, figuring that she could give most of them away as gifts.

She walked over to where she could pay for the items and Abbie had taken over that station. Eve handed her credit card over to Abbie, who thanked her for shopping at Bluebird Beauty. "I hope you have a great day."

"Actually, I have one question," Eve said. It was now or never. "I want to talk to you about something that happened about eighteen years ago, if that's okay with you. I'm a reporter from D.C., and I'm hoping to connect some dots based on some things I heard."

Eve could see the moment that Abbie realized what she was talking about because her eyes glazed over before she closed them. She took a deep breath and said, "I really don't talk about that anymore. Thank you so much for shopping here and I hope you stop by again."

A dejected Eve nodded her head, not wanting to push the woman further. "Thank you," she said as she grabbed her purchases and turned away. She was a couple of steps from the booth when she heard someone say her name. She turned back and was face-to-face with Abbie once more.

"Why do you want to talk to me about the accident?" she whispered.

"Because I think I might know who did it," Eve answered. "Now, I'm not one hundred percent sure."

"Oh, I know who did it."

"You do?"

Abbie tightened the bun on top of her head before putting her arms back down at her sides.

"Listen, how about you come over to my house on

Tuesday afternoon? School is in session and my husband is at work. That way we won't be interrupted."

"Sure," Eve said, and Abbie rattled off her address and number while Eve typed it on her phone.

"I'll see you then," she said before walking back to her shop.

Eve turned around, not believing how lucky she had been. She placed her phone back into her pocket and looked up and found Mayor Blake staring at her. Although she didn't know him well, she could tell that he didn't look happy.

20

———

Eve was disappointed as she read the text message on her phone. Abbie had to reschedule their meeting at her home because one of her children had come down with a cold.

"Do you want to play a board game?"

Eve had been relaxing but was willing to admit that she was bored. Her ears perked up at Kane's suggestion.

"What did you have in mind?"

"Hensley left Pandemic over here a few months ago when we tried hosting a family game night."

"Sure, that would be fun," Eve said as she uncrossed her legs and stood up. The next thing she heard had her dashing to Kane's side. The sound of glass shattering near the front of the home put Eve and Kane on high alert.

"It sounds like something broke a window at the front of the house."

"Or someone."

Kane grabbed Eve's hand and they walked toward the front door with him leading the way. Before Kane could turn on the lights, Eve thought she saw what looked to be a large stone on the floor in front of them. Someone smashed one of the windows of the door. When the lights flicked on, Eve confirmed that she was wrong. It was a brick on the floor. Kane saw the brick and sprinted toward the front door. He yanked it open and ran outside. From her position in the house, Eve could see him looking up and down the street. She assumed he was looking to see if he could find anything that might point to who threw the brick, and if they might still be near the house. Eve knelt down and picked up the brick.

Eve flipped it over and found a note stuck to the bottom. Being careful not to cut her fingers on the glass shards, she pulled the note from the brick and wiped it off. The note had her name on it. She unfolded the piece of paper and read the words on the page.

Stop your investigation now before someone gets hurt. This is your final warning.

The note was once again unsigned. She read it over a couple more times before Kane walked over the threshold.

"I'm gonna call Axel and have him come by and look at this," he said to her.

"Before you do that, here," she said, handing him the note.

"I think you and I need to talk."

"I agree but we need to get the police over here as soon as possible. Then we can talk."

"It's great that you guys are willing to file a police report. We can do some looking around and see who might have been in the area. We won't be able to find fingerprints on the brick, but maybe there's evidence on the note that was meant for Eve. We'll try our best to track down the culprits. Hopefully, they've left some clues behind."

She crossed her arms as Axel described what he thought would happen. It didn't surprise her that, although they could look into it, there wasn't much they could do right at this moment about the incident. But she knew that whoever was trying to stop her from following the trail of crumbs in D.C. had made their way to Capitol.

"Thanks for coming by." Kane said, walking his brother to the door.

"I'll let you know if I hear anything."

"Same goes over here." Kane closed the door and locked it before turning to face Eve. "You and I need to talk."

"I know, I know. We should probably heat up leftovers first though. Well, maybe I'm speaking for myself. Although I'm not hungry after all of this, I know I need to eat."

"Good point."

The duo walked back into the kitchen where Eve took out the stew she had made earlier in the week and split it between Kane and herself.

"I think you should stay in the house until we figure out what's going on."

"Kane, you can't keep me locked up in the house."

"If it keeps you safe, I will." Kane put the stew into the microwave without missing a beat.

"Keeping me safe is one thing. Locking me away is a totally different ballgame. I can take care of myself."

Kane closed the door and, before she knew it, had her cornered between his body and the countertop. Normally this would piss her off, but here she felt protected. She felt secure and that worried her. His words brought her out of her thoughts. "We aren't sure what's going on, and until we know, we need to make sure you're safe. Whoever this is left D.C. and came all the way here for you. That says a lot."

Eve knew he had a good point, although she didn't want to admit it. "Kane, I have no problem giving you a heads up, but you can't keep me locked away here. I need to be able to continue investigating and hopefully figure out whoever is doing this and why they're trying so hard to keep this secret buried."

Eve could see that Kane was tossing the idea around in his head. "Sounds like a plan, although I would prefer to be with you at all times." Given what was going on right now, Eve wouldn't mind him going everywhere with her either. "Eve, I know whatever we've been doing has been rocky, but I want you to know how much I care about you. This isn't about me trying to control what you do or how you want to do it."

Eve nodded, because she knew that's what the deal was. But she also knew that chances were this wouldn't stop whoever was coming after her.

"I know I'm harping on this because I can't keep you anywhere you don't want to be, but I think staying put might be the best bet."

"Are you going to stay with me at all times? How will this all work? Are you going to make this house more secure? Because someone literally just came up to your house and threw a brick at it."

Before Kane could respond Eve noticed that her hand was shaking as she brought it to her face. The almost car accident had rattled her and, while escaping D.C. had brought some ease to the danger, the fact that whoever was doing this found her in Capitol, a place she considered safe, threw her for a loop. Emotions that she didn't realize were there were bubbling up to the surface like a volcano ready to erupt.

Kane, noticing her distress, reached over and brought her into his arms. He whispered sweet nothings in her ear as they rocked back and forth in his kitchen. "Whenever you want to talk about this, I'm here, okay?"

Eve looked up at him and nodded. She knew that he knew some of the pieces of the puzzle, but she would need to sit down with him and lay everything out, including one of the reasons why she came to Capitol to begin with. She wasn't looking forward to that.

"How about this? We both lie low for a few days and see where things stand after that."

Eve thought it sounded like a good idea, although she wanted to wrap this up as quickly as possible. But what choice did she have? She wouldn't see Abbie until sometime the following week, so she didn't have much of a reason to leave the house without Kane. She could compromise on this for the next couple of days. "So, since it's almost the weekend and we aren't really venturing outside, what do you want to do?"

"I think we can think of something." Kane dug into the stew.

21

"Did I hear that right? A brick flew through Kane's window?"

Eve took her time catching Liv and Jules up on what had recently happened. "You heard that right. With a note with my name on it."

"Have the police mentioned anything? Any leads?" Eve could read the look of concern on Jules' face.

"Not one, which honestly was to be expected. It was always going to be harder to track this person down because we have nothing on video. Although he hasn't admitted this, I think Kane has taken this has a personal attack on himself because this happened while I was in his home. In related news, we've been taking matters in to our own hands." Eve paused for a moment. "Kane stepped up the security measures on his house and has kept me in his sight at all times. Which has been a blessing and a curse," Eve said, tapping her fingertips on the desk.

"Oh, really?" asked Liv, clearly picking up on the vibe Eve was laying down. "How freaky are you guys getting?"

"Liv!" Eve chuckled at Jules' exclamation.

"Uh-huh. And I won't get into too much detail about either. Just take my word for it. I haven't had this much sex ever, and it's been helpful in taking my mind off of things."

Although the chance of this news getting back to D.C. was slim, she felt the need to talk to her friends about it. Kane had done a lot to calm her down, but there was something about talking to her girlfriends that made everything better.

"I miss y'all so much. Hopefully, I'll be able to come back to D.C. soon."

Out of the corner of her eye, Eve saw Kane standing at her doorjamb with his arms crossed. Normally when he did that, it brought a sense of comfort, but this time things seemed tense.

"We miss you too. Do you have any idea when you'll be back?" Jules asked.

Eve's eyes didn't leave Kane's. "Uh, no I don't, but I have to go, okay?" She turned back to her laptop and flashed a quick smile.

"Okay. Let us know if we can do anything."

"Will do. Bye." She ended the call and turned her attention to Kane. "Is everything all right? Any word about who might have thrown the brick?"

They were a couple of days into their personal solaces and had only left Kane's house to grab groceries from the store.

"No. I came in here to do this." He stalked into the room and kissed Eve squarely on the lips. Eve's hands migrated down to his pants, brushing up against his member. Kane's quick intake of breath confirmed how much he wanted her. His hands slid down her body and cupped her thighs.

Sensing what he wanted, she let her legs go and they wrapped around his waist as he carried her across the hall to his bedroom. She wasn't sure how it happened, but somehow Kane's T-shirt went missing Where? Eve didn't know, nor did she care.

He pulled her focus once more when his hands ended up on her ass, cupping it as he held her up before tossing her onto the bed in the guest room. He didn't give her an inch of breathing room before he was on top of her, pulling her shirt over her head. He left kisses on her neck and collarbone, and, when he touched a specific spot on her neck, she gasped at the unexpected sensation. His kisses continued until they reached her lace-covered breasts, the red color popping against her light amber skin.

"I think red just became my favorite color."

Eve chuckled at Kane's words, but it soon turned into a moan as he continued on his mission to bring her pleasure. His body moved to line up with hers and, when his eyes met hers, the intensity in them almost caused her to combust. His lips ended up back on hers as his hands undid her bra and, one by one, removed the straps from her shoulders. Once the bra fell on the floor, her breasts were the only things on his mind; all of his attention focused on bringing her nipples to hardened peaks.

Although Eve loved what Kane was doing to her breasts, she wanted more. She was ready to feel their bodies touch with nothing between them. When they both removed their pants and his hands were playing with her matching lacy panties, Eve wanted to wrap her legs around him again, begging him to take her to where they both wanted to go. He shifted her panties to the side and inserted two fingers into her, and Eve about lost her mind. She was twisting and turning on the bed, unable to control her body's movements given the pleasant torture.

"I need you. Now."

"Is that right?" he asked. "I want to get you off first." And that was when he began alternating between his fingers and tongue. When Eve went over the edge, Kane continued his assault, revving her up for the next one. Eve was still riding high on her orgasm and the next thing she knew, Kane was teasing his condom-covered cock at her entrance, rubbing it up and down her seam. He inserted himself in her with one thrust, causing Eve's eyes to roll into the back of her head.

"This isn't going to be slow," Kane warned as he thrust into her once more.

"I don't care," Eve said, finally finding some words to speak.

"Excellent."

Eve thought she could predict his movements, but the way he changed up his thrusts made her body lose control even more. She could tell he was affected, too, based on how frantic his movements became. He was losing control too.

"I'm getting close," she heard him say, but what he did next surprised her. He pulled all the way out and said, "Get on your hands and knees."

Eve froze. She wasn't used to following directions from anyone in her personal life, so her immediate reaction was to pause. His words had taken her by surprise, but she was also shocked that she liked it. "How long had you been waiting to say that?"

"Longer than I care to admit." His words were followed by a groan, sending a shiver through her body.

She debated keeping him waiting a bit longer, but wondered why she should torture them both? Eve rose on to all fours and he entered her from behind, causing a slew of needs and desires to course through her. She met his measured thrusts and soon she was crossing the finish line, followed closely by him.

A few minutes later, Eve and Kane crawled into her bed, a change in scenery from the nights they spent in his bedroom.

He pulled the covers over them and Eve into his arms. It didn't take long for Eve to settle her head on his chest near his heart, where she could hear and feel it beat hard.

"Did you like that?"

"Mmhmm?" Eve was happy she could get that noise out because her brain wasn't processing much at the moment.

"I was a little more... bossy for lack of a better word."

Eve replayed the moment in her mind once more and smiled. "I liked it a lot. More than I care to admit."

Kane chuckled because she threw his words back at him. "I'm glad. I didn't want to do anything that made you uncomfortable."

She smiled. "If I was uncomfortable, I would have said something. I hadn't been expecting it, but was very turned on by it."

"I'm glad," he whispered as he leant up. She met his lips for a quick kiss and placed her head back down on his chest.

As his heartbeat slowly returned to normal, Eve wondered what they were going to do when the little bubble they had created in Capitol was broken and they both had to go back to D.C. Did he see her as a part of his life, or would whatever this was be destined to end when they left Capitol?

22

———

"Kane?" Eve called out. She had woken up in her bed all alone. She reached over and checked her phone; she had about two hours before she needed to go to talk to Abbie.

Eve got up and headed to the bathroom to take a shower. Once she was ready to go, she wandered downstairs but still didn't see Kane. She walked to the front of the house and saw both vehicles still outside.

She headed to the basement and heard Kane on the phone. Figuring it wasn't worth it to disturb him, she sent him a brief text, letting him know she was going to be out but would be back in a couple of hours. Eve grabbed her things she needed for the interview and headed to the SUV.

Twenty minutes later, Eve sat in the vehicle outside of a charming house that was not too far from Capitol Diner. She turned off the car and grabbed the keys along with her book bag before exiting. She was ready to have this discussion with Abbie, or so she thought. She looked at her surroundings, making sure that no one was around to see where she was going. Although Kane had warned her about going places alone, she knew this was something that she needed to do, and it needed to happen fast.

Eve adjusted one of her book bag straps and walked up the pathway to the house before knocking on the door.

"Come in!" she heard, and she turned a doorknob into the residence. If there was one word to describe Abbie's house, she would say it was *homey*. The hallway was lined with pictures of Abbie and her family. If Eve didn't know that Abbie had children, she would have been clued in based on the toys lying around in the living room.

"Hey, thanks for coming. I'm sorry I had to reschedule our meeting from last week. It made little sense to do it if I had a sick kid, and I didn't want to get you sick," Abbie said as she entered the hallway.

"Oh, no worries, it's fine. I appreciate you inviting me into your home."

"Do you want something to eat or drink? Come, follow me." Abbie led the way as the two women walked into her living room. They sat down on the couch before Abbie jumped back up. "Oh, I meant to get you something. Do you need anything to eat or drink? Wait, I already asked you that." Abbie shook her head at herself. "Sorry, I have mom brain sometimes and I forget what I'm doing."

"Oh no, I'm fine and no worries," Eve replied. "You have a lovely home."

"Thanks so much. It's actually cleaner than it normally is, but that's because the kids are in school right now and I have more time to put things away."

"How many kids do you have?"

Abbie smiled, and Eve assumed she was thinking about

them. "Two. Annie is six and Tommy is four." She told Eve about her children and husband, Tim. Eve enjoyed the conversation and hoped that this would relax her a bit. Although Eve was nervous, she couldn't imagine how Abbie was feeling, and debated how much she was going to share with a complete stranger.

"Okay. So, you came to discuss what happened to me eighteen years ago." Eve appreciated that Abbie didn't want to pull any punches.

"Yes, I do, if that's okay with you. And if you don't mind, I'd like to record our conversation."

"You're more than welcome to." Abbie closed her eyes for a moment and took a deep breath. "You would think that after all these years it would be easier to tell the story."

"No, actually, I don't. It was a very traumatic event where you could have been permanently hurt, and they never caught the person who did it. I can only imagine what trauma you went through. So no, I don't expect it to get that much easier to talk about."

Abbie's eyes met Eve's and Eve could see the tears glistening in them.

"I think I know the basics of what happened," Eve said, trying to make sure that her tone and words were measured. "What I want to know is who did it. I have some suspicions."

Abbie swallowed hard. "So, I know who it was because I saw them. But I knew no one would believe me if I went public."

"Who hit you all those years ago, Abbie?"

Abbie brushed her hair behind her ear and looked down at her feet before looking back at Eve. "Anthony Blake. Well, now Representative Anthony Blake, and it wasn't an accident."

"How do you know it wasn't an accident?"

"Because he threatened me before it happened."

That bombshell left Eve stunned. "But—"

Abbie's eyes met Eve's and a tear flowed from her face. "I also know it was him because he stopped and checked on me before he drove off."

That comment was enough to send Eve's mind spinning. "You've got to be shitting me. Excuse my language."

"My children have heard worse, I assure you." The tears were free flowing from Abbie at this point and Eve laid a hand on her shoulder, trying to provide some comfort to the stranger who was pouring her heart out. Abbie turned toward her, and Eve placed her arms around her, pulling her into an embrace. Eve could only imagine how hard it was for her to tell this story even if everything had taken place years ago. Plus, she had kept the secret of who the assailant was for so long, Eve could only imagine how that felt as well.

Eve gently rubbed her back, hoping to provide some comfort to the upset woman. "Do you want to continue?" Abbie sniffled and tried to wipe her eyes, but she didn't answer. Eve knew the professional barrier that she tried to maintain had been thrown out of the window. She looked around the room and saw some tissues on the dining room table. "I'm going to walk over to your dining room table so I can get you some tissues."

All Abbie did was nod her head, giving Eve the go ahead. She got up and walked over to grab the tissues and dashed back to the couch, handing Abbie the tissues to wipe her face. It didn't take long for Abbie to pull herself together and she bundled the tissues up into a ball in her hand and leaned back on to her couch. "Sorry. I didn't expect that to happen."

"Don't worry about it. Totally understandable given the circumstances. Once again, if you don't want to continue, please just let me know."

Abbie shook her head. "No, it's okay. I want to continue. I didn't expect to be this upset over this still." She sniffled once more.

"Why did he threaten you?"

Abbie crossed her legs and brushed her hands against her thighs.

"I overheard something that I wasn't meant to."

"Welcome to the club." Eve quickly filled her in on what happened to her back in D.C.

"The information I overheard was about Mayor Blake, before he became mayor. He had come in to eat dinner with someone and left the diner without incident. Around the time he went outside, I went out to take my break. Another man was threatening Mayor Blake, so I stepped back into the doorway while the man yelled at him. I think he owed someone a lot of money. Once the man sped off, I came out and asked if I should call the police. Mayor Blake told me it was best if I acted like this never happened and walked away. I didn't say a word to anyone, yet that was not enough because I ended up in the hospital. Now, do I know if the two are related? No."

"Do you want the truth about what happened to you out there?"

"I do. And deep down, I want Anthony to pay for what he did to me."

"I can do that if you're okay with me writing this article."

Abbie nodded her head but said nothing. Her eyes looked downward, almost as if she was lost in thought.

"Would you be willing to come forward and tell your side of the story?"

"Oh, no." Abbie shook her head viciously. "It could mean that I am putting my family in danger. It also happened so long ago, and everyone has moved on."

"Have you?"

"Have I what?"

"Moved on."

Eve saw some doubt in her eyes before she dipped her head. "Yes. I had to. I mostly just avoid the mayor and Representative Blake whenever we're in the same place. We might say hello if it can't be avoided, but that's it. I prefer it that way. They leave me alone and I leave them alone."

"I want to say again that if you want to stop this conversation at any point, that's completely fine."

Abbie took a deep breath and said, "Is this going to be a hard question to answer?"

"I hope not, but I know that this conversation has dug up some memories that you've probably tried your best to keep buried." Eve paused to gauge Abbie's reaction. So far, she looked okay given that she had cried moments before, but Eve hesitated to drop the hammer. "How was your recovery?"

The shaky breath that Abbie took told Eve that her question brought up memories buried long ago.

"It was a long road of hospitalization and rehab, but I made it through. I definitely have my family to thank for helping me. It's also how I met my husband."

"Oh really?" Eve hoped she would elaborate to because

she was curious and she hoped it would take Abbie's mind off of the tragic memories that she was reliving.

Abbie smiled before she spoke. "My husband was bringing his mother to her therapy appointment and he held the door for me as I was leaving. My parents were supposed to come and pick me up but they were running late so he ended up making sure that his mother was ready for her appointment and rushed back outside to see if I was still there. And I was. He asked me for my number that day and the rest is history." The smile dimmed on her face. "There were a lot of barriers that my husband had to break and help me with, mostly due to the accident, but he has never left my side. We've been together ever since. It's part of the reason why I would never wish away what happened to me. It made me who I am today, and I met the love of my life because of it."

Eve swallowed hard as she listened to Abbie's words. Abbie's comments gave Eve a lot to think about. "Thanks for telling me your story. If there is anything you don't want mentioned in the article, please let me know and I'll share the rough draft with you. I want to take as many precautions with your story as I possibly can."

"Thank you for listening. And for believing me."

"Of course. And if you want to come forward with your story, please let me know."

Abbie offered a small smile but didn't respond. Abbie walked Eve to the door and told her, "Thanks for coming." Once Eve was outside, she heard the door click behind her. Eve walked back to the SUV and, once she was locked inside the vehicle, she felt safe from the outside world. She dug into her book bag and pulled out her phone. She saw that she had several messages and calls from Kane. She found his number and called him back without checking them. She heard the click letting her know that the call had connected, but Kane said nothing.

"Kane, I know you're there."

"Where are you?"

The harshness of his tone took her by surprise. "I went to chat with someone, but I'm on my way back now."

She heard him let go of a breath that he had been holding in. "I almost started searching for you."

His voice dripped with concern; she knew she had put it there. "Kane, I'm sorry. I sent you a text message letting you know I was headed out and would be back in an hour."

"Yeah, it's been about two hours since that message."

Eve looked down at the center console and realized he was right. "Oh no, I'm sorry. Time flew by and I just got caught up."

"It's fine. Are you headed back now?"

"Yes. I'm already in the SUV, about to pull off."

"Good."

"I'll see you in about twenty minutes."

"See you soon."

With that, Kane hung up. Maybe interrupting his call would have been a better way to go about this.

It didn't take long for Eve to drive back to Kane's house. When she arrived, he was waiting for her on his porch.

"Eve, I was worried about you." His words and the tone of his voice told her that that was true and increased the guilt she felt about not being fully transparent at a time like this. He didn't say another word, but held her in his arms, reassuring himself that she was with him and safe and sound.

23

"Eve, I thought I told you not to bring anything? You're a guest."

The following Saturday was the day of the food drive that Capitol Diner was hosting. "I had to bring something, so I figured some canned goods and other nonperishable items would be a delightful addition. Plus, I made some of my mom's secret peach cobbler and brought it to the barbecue for folks to enjoy."

"That's so sweet of you, dear. I'll take that from you. Why don't you go join the others in the back? It's straight down that hallway and through the door at the end. Where's Kane?"

"Axel grabbed him as soon as we pulled up."

"Those boys." Rose shook her head with a smile. "I assume Axel dragged Kane back there."

Rose gestured to the hallway behind her. Eve smiled as the older woman took the dish from her and placed it on the countertop. She then followed Rose's directions and walked down the hallway. She opened the back door, strolled out onto the porch, and leaned on the banister overlooking the backyard. Although Eve's first instinct was to find Kane in the crowd of people near the bonfire, the expansive size of the backyard overrode the thought. She stayed put. The backyard seemed to go on for miles, but, if Eve squinted, she thought she could see another home in the distance.

"Lovely evening, isn't it?"

Eve turned toward the voice and found Mayor Blake standing a short distance away. Where had he come from? Was he trying to sneak up on her? Although their other encounters had been cordial, Eve's gut told her there was something different about this.

"Yes, it is, Mayor Blake. Perfect night to have this get-together."

"Have you been enjoying Capitol so far?"

Eve nodded her head. "This town is lovely, and everyone has been so welcoming." She glanced at him once more. The smile he gave her didn't quite reach his eyes. It was the fake politician smile she was used to seeing in D.C., when she caught someone she was interviewing in a lie. He moved closer to her and leaned on the banister.

Mayor Blake didn't respond right away. She looked over her shoulder and found him staring at her. Intently.

"I heard that you've been going to the library fairly frequently."

She had been to the library three times since she arrived in Capitol. "I didn't know that was something noteworthy. After all, I am a journalist." She could feel herself channeling her inner Liv and did her best to tamp down the words she wanted to say.

"Be very careful about what you're doing. You never know if it might turn around and bite you in the—"

"Everything all right over here, Mayor?" Eve could hear the warning in Kane's tone, but it had a different effect on her. Kane's voice floated over her like a warm embrace. A sense of comfort she didn't know she needed. She'd save the analysis of her feelings for later.

"Yes, everything is fine. I was asking Eve about how she was enjoying her time here, that's all." Eve made note of what he conveniently left out.

"I'm sure that was all. Ma was looking for you to make a speech or somethin'." The expression on Mayor Blake's face did a complete one-eighty. The fake politician smile was plastered on his face again and he went on his way.

"Are you all right?"

"Yeah, I'm fine. That isn't the first weird encounter I've had with a politician in my lifetime. Why?"

"I was waiting for you to come over and spotted him talking to you. He seemed to be a little too close for comfort."

"You've been watching me? From where? I didn't see you."

He pointed to where a group of people were standing. "Axel, some of my high school friends, and I were talking over there and I saw you when you walked out of the house. Then I saw the mayor make a beeline over to you."

"Uh-huh," Eve said before she walked away from the banister and headed to the stairs. She wanted to make it over to his brother and friends. Kane followed closely behind her, so close that the hairs on her arm stood at attention.

Before they reached his friends, Kane whispered in her ear, "I think you and I need to talk."

Eve turned around and whispered, "I think we've done a

lot of talking, more talking over the time I've been here than we had since you snuck back into my life."

Kane let out a dry chuckle. "I hardly snuck back into your life, but it is about the mayor."

Eve froze for a second. "Can this wait until we get home?" Eve said nothing about the fact that she had called his place home and hoped he hadn't noticed.

"Yes, it can wait until we get home." His emphasis on the word *home* told her he had. And the peck he laid on her lips in a public setting sealed the deal.

"THANKS FOR COMING WITH ME TONIGHT." Eve looked over at Kane, verifying that he had said the words. They spent most of the drive back in silence, and, honestly, that was how Eve had preferred it. If they said nothing to each other, words wouldn't fly, and feelings wouldn't be hurt. Or so she thought.

"Of course! Why wouldn't I be there?"

"I didn't know if you were too caught up in trying to talk to Abbie Henderson that you would have made time."

Eve's eyes darted over to Kane. She noticed the obvious dig but didn't respond.

"Speechless?"

"Kane, I don't know why you're being an ass about this."

This time he didn't respond as his hands gripped the wheel tighter. The rest of the car ride was silent outside of the low humming of the music on the radio. Once Kane put the pickup truck in park in his driveway, Eve flung the door open and hopped out without waiting for him to come around and help her. He followed her up to the house where she patiently waited for him to open the door before stepping inside. Once he had closed the front door, he turned to Eve. She folded her arms across her chest, bracing for an argument.

"What the hell was that?"

"What the hell was what, Kane?"

"Why has Mayor Blake taken a special interest in you? Based on what I walked up on, I assume he wasn't too happy that you showed up at the food drive tonight." Eve didn't respond, further aggravating Kane. "Talk to me, Eve."

"What is there to say?"

"How about the truth?"

"The truth? We can talk about who is telling the truth." Eve didn't go any further because Kane looked uncomfortable; her comment had landed the way she wanted it to. They both had been less than forthcoming with one another. He didn't have a reason to be angry with her when he was guilty of the same thing. At least that was the reasoning in her mind.

"We both need to talk to one another, but can we break out the whiskey first?"

Eve knew this was going to be a long night. She went into the kitchen, and Kane followed behind her. He reached into his liquor cabinet, pulled out a bottle of whiskey, and grabbed a cup of glasses.

"Do you want it straight?"

"Yes," she said before he poured the whiskey into his glass. "Definitely something strong if we are going to make it through this conversation."

Kane poured the liquid into the glass. He handed it to her and the two of them walked into the living room and sat down on the couch. She folded her feet underneath her as she cradled the glass.

"So, I think you need to tell me everything."

Eve threw her head back and closed her eyes, still holding the glass in her hand. "If I tell you everything you need to tell me why you take those late-night calls. Whenever someone sends you a text you head downstairs to your study."

"Now, this isn't about me."

"Yes, it is. If you want to have an open discussion, every-thing needs to be on the table." She took a sip of the whiskey and was happy to feel the slight burn in the back of her throat as it went down.

"Deal."

Kane's response shocked Eve because she wasn't expecting him to be forthcoming.

"How much do you know about Congressman Anthony Blake?"

"Are you really going to start this with a question for me?"

Eve sighed. "Humor me."

"He's a few years older than me, so we didn't run in the same crowd. We have run into each other many times here and in D.C. Why?"

Might as well pull the Band-Aid off. "I think the congressman was somehow involved in the accident that injured Abbie Henderson. Scratch that, I know he's involved."

Kane sat up straight and threw his hands into his hair. He pulled at the strands before he said, "You've gotta be shitting me."

"I wish I were."

"You know that if you're wrong—"

"I'm not wrong. I know what I heard, and I know what my sources have told me. Plus, someone doesn't want me digging deeper into this because they keep trying to harm me. Does that sound like someone wrong to you?"

"That came out wrong. I'm sorry. I'm just—" He cut himself off before he could finish his thought.

"What?" Eve whispered. She had a feeling she knew what he was going to say but wanted to hear it from his lips.

"Whatever we find out about Blake is going to have implications not only here but in Washington. And I'm sure the Blakes know some heavy hitters who would do anything to keep this quiet." He raked another hand through his hair. "Is this why you think you're being targeted?"

Eve dipped her head and took another sip from her glass. "Ah. Happy to confirm that for you. So how are you involved in this?"

"What?"

"I'm not the only who was keeping secrets here." Eve could feel some of her anger rising to the surface. She took a deep breath, trying to calm the emotions that threatened to take over. "I know you're involved in this somehow and that you've been following what I've been doing."

"How do you know that?"

"Since we're being honest, I saw some tabs you had open on your computer the day Hensley came over and invited me to Captain's Bar. You told me I could go down to your study to work if I wanted to and—"

"And you saw what was on my computer screen?"

Eve shrugged. "Basically. I saw the articles on your screen and they included ones I wrote that had nothing to do with Representative Blake."

"Part of that was because your writing interested me."

"The other part?" She wasn't letting him off the hook either.

"This stays off the record, right?"

Eve was taken aback. "Of course. Why would you think—"

"That wasn't meant to offend you. I want to make sure we are on the same page because I'm about to reveal some things that can't leave this conversation."

Eve bit her lip. His trust and whatever it was that they were doing meant more to her than a headline or a story. "Okay, spill."

"I was trying to figure out what you were trying to connect him to. Didn't start connecting the dots until I saw you talking to Abbie Henderson at the Founder's Day Fair. I assume that's where you went the afternoon I didn't hear from you."

Eve nodded. "So, what do you have to do with this? Be straight with me." A mixture of emotions bubbled to the surface. She was annoyed that he was upset with her about hiding things when he had done the same thing and wondered what all of this meant for their future...if there was one. She was also curious about what she suspected was a figurative bomb he was about to drop.

Kane licked his lips before he replied, "Before Flint and I started Homes for Vets, I worked for a top-secret security firm called Knox. I still do work for them occasionally, hence the messages that are sometimes sent in the middle of the night."

Eve didn't know what she had been expecting, but it wasn't that, even with hints from Rae and Flint. "Was Flint ever involved in this?"

Kane shook his head. "No, Flint wasn't recruited to work for them, but he knows some of the people that work for the security firm. Part of that is because his brother works for them."

"Wait a minute... Garrett, right? Garrett works for Knox? Does Flint know anything about that? Hell, do the Wests know anything about it?"

"Honestly, Flint might know, given the fact that someone might have tried to leak it during his campaign, but I don't think all of the Wests know. Flint mentioned that he told Rae a little bit about what I do, but I don't think he delved into details. Most of that is because he doesn't know much about it either to be frank."

"You are being pretty sparse on the details."

"It's all I can share at this time."

Eve nodded. Although she wanted to know more, she understood why he had to hold back on some things, much like she had to hold back on some of the details related to her job, whether it was keeping a source protected or preventing some information from making it into an article, to avoid getting sued.

"I almost feel as if I were still more involved with Knox, I wouldn't have let my guard down and we would, without a doubt, know who threw the brick at my house."

Eve took a step closer and put her hand on Kane's cheek. "Don't blame yourself for what happened because it wasn't your fault. We can assume that it was someone related to the Blakes who did it."

"Why did you leave out the real reason you wanted to come to Capitol?" Kane's sudden question took her by surprise. She removed her hand from his cheek and guessed they were ready to lay everything out on the table.

"Because I didn't want to involve you even more than you are already." Eve could feel anger radiating off of Kane. He clenched and unclenched his left hand while his right rubbed the back of his neck.

"I thought you'd trust me by now." His words came out even, a stark contrast to the emotions playing out on his face. But it didn't scare Eve. She was ready to face whatever feelings he was dealing with head on. He didn't like the fact that he was now the one in the dark, versus him keeping Knox a secret from her.

"I do to a certain extent."

"What do you mean to a certain extent?"

Eve glanced down at her hands before making their way back up to his face. "Kane, you've refused to tell me what you do outside of working for your foundation. Full and undivided trust is scarce for both of us, seeing as how we're just now coming clean with a whole lot of shit. Looks like you don't like when the tables are turned huh?"

Eve knew her parting shot was more emotionally charged than anything and that she shouldn't have said it; it only fed the flame of their emotions. She could feel the tension beaming off of Kane before he stood up and announced that he was going outside. He walked out the front door and closed it without saying another word. To be honest, she was happy he left, giving them both some time to cool down.

In part, he would be more affected by the outcome of this than her. His and his family's life in Capitol, and his life in

D.C., would be turned upside down forever. For his sake, she couldn't afford to be wrong, but she had heard what she heard, and she believed Abbie's story. Deep down she knew she wasn't wrong. It was only a matter of time before this information was released or they shut her up for good.

24

Eve didn't wait to see how long Kane stayed outside to get some fresh air. She finished the whiskey and went upstairs. After their conversation, she wanted a bit of space; she returned to the guest room for the first time in days.

She stripped herself of the clothes she had worn to the food drive and hopped into the shower. What was there left to do? Based on what she knew, everything was hearsay unless Abbie came forward. If she offered the information she had, the Blakes could deny it and she would get laughed out of Capitol and potentially out of D.C.

Her instincts told her she would never forget this case or what happened, but was she willing to risk her career for it? Heck, she might even get sued for defamation of character. She could write the article and just not hit publish. After all, she needed to update Casey on her progress.

She decided to write an article based on what she knew. She would avoid direct quotes from Abbie. She didn't want to force a victim to live through her trauma once again if she could avoid it. With a plan set in place, Eve finished her shower.

Her thoughts wandered to Kane once more as she tried to guess what he might be up to right now. Had he come back inside? Was he asleep in his bed? She figured he hadn't gone out on a drive because that would mean leaving her alone in the house. Even though she could find out where he was and what he was doing, she didn't. She thought they both needed time to cool off and to be by themselves.

Sometimes being alone was an opportunity to examine a situation along with one's own thoughts and actions. This was where Eve was. The time she spent with Kane in Capitol had been magical. Eve would say that the time spent in their own little bubble had allowed them to get to know each other on a personal level, but there was hurt on both sides from not being up front about the projects they were working on. Where did they go from here? Where did they go when they returned to D.C.?

Eve rubbed her chin with her thumb and index finger, and she tried to figure out what a path forward looked like. Part of her wanted to focus on the Blake story because, as of right now, that seemed to be the easier thing to deal with. Her emotions were tied up in whatever was going on with Kane, clouding her judgment. What did she want from Kane? What did he want from her? She stopped herself from going to ask him because—she still agreed with her original stance— some time apart would be good for the both of them.

So that meant Eve had plenty of time to write, and she got to work.

~

EVE HAD FALLEN asleep with her laptop in the bed, draft article still open. She stretched and checked the time on her laptop. It was after 10:00; she realized that she had slept in and needed to get up. After a stretch of her arms above her head, she got out of bed and headed to the stairs. Before she could hit the first step, she felt a strong urge to look into Kane's bedroom where they had spent many nights pleasuring one another. She glanced into the room, fearful that he might see her looking in. But he wasn't there. She stood at the top of his stairs in silence, searching for a clue as to where he was in the house. Hearing nothing, she bounded down the stairs.

The urge to have a sip of coffee was powerful. When Eve entered the kitchen, she noticed a coffeepot was still there, but the coffee was now cold. She moved quickly to make another, and Eve found it a little funny how used to his kitchen she was now. She had definitely made herself at home and was a little worried about what would happen when this all ended.

Waiting for her coffee provided an opportunity to check her phone for emails. Once that was completed, she grabbed her cup of coffee and walked to the front of the house. One quick look out of the window showed that Kane was in the house somewhere because both cars were still parked in the driveway. She would bet her salary that he was in the study working. Part of her wanted to go downstairs and talk to him, but she was scared. Scared of what they both might say, scared of what decisions they might make about the rest of her time in Capitol and what they wanted to do when they got back to D.C.

Eve ran back up the stairs into the guest room with a

newfound determination to finish the article. Once she sat down at the desk, Eve told herself that she knew what she had to do. She couldn't let this go and knew that she was putting a lot of things on the line, but she also knew she couldn't live with herself if she let this secret stay buried.

"ARE YOU HUNGRY?"

Eve hadn't heard Kane approach her door, let alone lean on the doorjamb with his arms crossed. Although he didn't look too happy, she was glad that he asked about food. As if on cue, Eve's stomach growled, leading to light laughter between the couple.

"I'll take that as a yes. How about I order takeout?"

"Sounds good."

"Is pizza okay?"

Eve nodded. "I usually like cheese or pepperoni and sausage."

"Pepperoni and sausage, it is."

This was the first time they'd had a conversation in hours, and Eve didn't realize how much she had missed it. She got the feeling that Kane missed it too because, while he was on his phone ordering the pizza, he walked into the guest room and leaned on the wall across from her desk. She watched him as he typed on his phone and once he was done, he placed the phone in his pocket.

"Dinner should be here in thirty to forty minutes."

"I can't believe it's already dinnertime. Where did the time go?"

"Time flies when you're busy. What are you working on?"

Eve debated showing him what she was working on. But they were turning over this whole new leaf being truthful to one another, so she figured what was the harm in doing so.

"I'm writing an article that's based on what I found out about the crime Blake committed eighteen years ago." It was the first time that she had referred to him by just his last name. Although it felt strange, she felt that he really didn't deserve the title of being a representative of the people of Capitol. Then again, who was she to judge?

"Mmhmm," Kane said, but he didn't elaborate. He leaned over her shoulder and started reading the article. "Sounds good so far. It'll be a great read for sure."

"Thanks."

"I'll let you keep at it and call you when the pizza arrives, okay?"

Eve nodded. "Thanks."

Although she wanted to think about their interaction, she had work to do. Letters turned into words; words turned into sentences; sentences turned into paragraphs. Eve spent the next few hours finishing up a draft of an article that she debated sending to Casey. She knew she needed to send something in because otherwise all her time in Capitol would have been for naught.

Kane brought two slices of pizza up for her when it arrived. He also brought up the soda that he kept stocked in the fridge just for her. Once she was done with this article, she knew that she had to make time to talk to him about everything. She didn't want to keep having to deal with what-ifs and maybes or the tension that still existed between them. Now, sexual tension was fine, but the uncertainty between them was a big problem, at least for her.

She went over her work once more before typing up an email to Casey, explaining what was going on regarding Abbie. Once that was sent off, she grabbed her plate and the soda can and headed downstairs. She was shocked to find Kane in the kitchen, loading dishes into the dishwasher. Although she thought she was prepared for this moment, he had surprised her. She had assumed he would be down in his study like he usually was. There was no way she could hide from him standing in front of the sink; she had nowhere else she could go. They were going to hash this out right now.

"I can wash this," she said as he looked over at her, his first acknowledgment that she had entered the room.

"No, just put it in the sink. I'll toss it into the dishwasher."

Eve shrugged and did as he asked. She tipped her can over into the sink, draining it of any liquid that might have remained before tossing it in the recycling bin.

"Kane, I think we should talk." There. She made the first move.

"I'm glad it's coming from you this time and not from me. But I agree. We need to talk."

"I'll sit out on the couch while you finish this up and we can do it then, unless you're busy with something else."

"Nope. I'll be done with this in about five minutes."

True to his word, Kane was done within five minutes and joined Eve on the couch. She was watching the local news broadcast but turned it off so that her full and undivided attention was on Kane.

"Thank you for inviting me to stay with you in Capitol. I have learned so much, met so many new people, and I've had a great time here. Well, besides the brick being thrown through your window." Eve scratched a small spot on her cheek before she continued. "Your hometown is beautiful."

"I'm glad you've enjoyed it." That's all Kane was going to give her.

"Kane, my gut tells me I'm not wrong about Representative Blake. I know what I heard. I know what Abbie told me, and I believe her."

Kane shifted his body to face Eve. "I believe you both too."

Some pressure that Eve put on herself lessened when she processed Kane's words. "The issue is whether to come forward though."

"Definitely, and without Abbie."

"What are you thinking?" Kane asked, breaking the silence between them.

Eve said nothing right away, taking that time to sort the jumbled ideas in her brain. "I think I still need to move forward with going public with this. The residents of Capitol deserve to know. The draft article I sent to Abbie and then to Casey goes into detail about what happened but doesn't out anyone."

"So, are you thinking about publishing the article to get the word out there?"

Eve rubbed a hand across her eyes. "Maybe? I assume it would end up being a national story so word would get back to everyone in Capitol. And that's if Casey even deems the article acceptable. I don't want lawsuits to occur because of all of this." She placed a hand on Kane's knee, but said nothing else. They still hadn't figured out where they stood with one another. When he laid his hand on top of hers, she felt somewhat reassured but not completely at ease.

"What if I told you I had an idea about how you could make a public splash about all of this?"

That got Eve's attention. "What are you thinking?"

"What if word on the street was that Representative Blake was getting ready to host a meet-and-greet type of event just before he goes back to D.C., and his team is working on how to pull everything together for it right now?"

"Seriously?" Kane nodded. "How do you know all of this?"

"Ma may or may not be catering the event."

"Is she, or isn't she?"

"She is."

"Well, that might give us something to work with." The wheels in Eve's head were turning, but she pumped the brakes on her thoughts about Representative Blake. "There's something else that needs to be worked out, and I'm not sure where to begin with that."

The shift in Kane's eyes told her he knew what she was talking about.

"I think we need to talk about us," said Eve.

"Eve, I've cared about you for a long time. I wouldn't have offered to have you come and stay out here with me if I didn't. I was upset that you didn't tell me the entire story about what you suspected regarding Anthony, but I understand your resistance."

"Yeah, I was worried about potentially throwing you in harm's way and hurting your work life in D.C. and you and your family's lives in Capitol."

Kane threw an arm around her shoulders and pulled her into his embrace. "I know. But I also want you to know that you don't have to do this or anything else alone. All of us involved in this are grown, and I'm sure I can at least speak for my family in that we want to stand for what's right. It's about time everyone knows who hurt Abbie, and it will all be thanks to you."

That vote of confidence made Eve's heart soar. She debated continuing the conversation to ask more about what they were going to do once they returned to D.C., but she thought there would be plenty of time to discuss that. Right now, she needed to focus on creating a plan to expose Representative Anthony Blake and showcase the man that he truly was.

25

A sudden knock on the door made Eve sit up, breaking the embrace that she and Kane were sharing. "Were you expecting anyone?"

It was a couple of days after their talk about what to do about Representative Blake. Eve and Kane had spent most of their time either working on their separate work projects or spending time with one another.

"I don't think so," he replied, but his tone said that something was up. "Why don't you answer it?"

She squinted her eyes at him as she stood up and headed toward the front door. She peeked outside through the new glass that had been installed after the brick incident. Eve let out a squeal before flicking the lock and opening the door.

"Jules! What are you doing here?"

"I'm here to support you, and I can't wait to see you in action tomorrow. It would look a little bad if Rae came down because Flint is a sitting congressman, and you know it's hard for Liv to break away because wedding season is picking back up. But I was so happy when Kane invited me."

Eve looked over her shoulder and found Kane with one hand in his pocket. He smiled at both women. "He really has a knack for knowing just what I need and when." Eve turned back around to look at Jules. "There's so much I need to catch you up on."

"Well, I'm here to help in any way I can." Eve pulled Jules's suitcase over the threshold. Once her things were in Kane's house, Eve reached over to give her friend a hug.

"Oh, I didn't know how much I missed you until just now. Wait. That's a lie. Video chats, phone calls, or text messages are nothing compared to seeing each other in person."

Jules squeezed a little tighter and said, "I completely agree. We've all missed you so much. Rae and Liv want to know how everything is going, especially what happens when you bust his chops."

"Duly noted."

"Why don't you ladies head into the kitchen and I'll bring Jules's stuff upstairs?" Kane asked as he walked up to the two women standing near his front door. He placed a hand on Eve's lower back and looked into her eyes.

Eve nodded and grinned at him. Kane smiled back before Eve led Jules into the kitchen. "Would you like anything to eat or drink? I think we have plenty to eat and I know we have water, soda, wine, and—"

"You seem awfully comfy here," Jules said, interrupting Eve. "Definitely the hostess with the mostest right now."

"You really need to stop hanging out with Liv." Eve opened the fridge and glanced inside. "And I do feel comfortable here."

"Well, you guys are coming back to D.C. soon, right?"

"Uh-huh. I informed Casey about what I knew, so I must

head back to D.C. for all the hoopla this is going to cause. I assume I'll be doing interviews and things of that nature because this is such a big deal. So, who knows what happens then." Eve closed the fridge and turned back to Jules.

"What do you mean, what happens then? Are you in Kane going to continue doing..." Jules trailed off before continuing, "Whatever it is you're doing?"

Eve sighed. "I don't know. To be honest, I haven't talked to him about it. I know that eventually he wants to move here full-time. My work is in D.C."

"Well," she said, propping a hip against the counter. "He's not moving here now, and you don't know where you'll both be in the next few years."

"That's a good point, and I know it doesn't hurt to talk to him about it. Doesn't mean I'm not worried about the outcome of that conversation. I've been super busy with everything involving Blake. I guess my conversation with Kane is long overdue. I have been putting it on the back burner." Eve knew deep down this was the case, but it was her first time admitting it out loud. She heard Kane start to come back down the stairs and turned her attention to Jules. "So, did you want something to drink?"

"A glass of water would be great." Eve walked to the cabinet, pulled a glass and asked, "Ice or no ice?"

"Ice is fine."

By the time she was handing Jules her glass of water, Kane came downstairs into the kitchen.

"Do y'all want to head to the diner and get something to eat?"

Eve's eyes widened. "Oh, you're gonna love Capitol Diner. Kane's mom owns it and she's the sweetest person."

"I'd love to go."

Eve brought Jules upstairs to show her where she would be staying and to give her a few minutes to unpack and freshen up. When she knew that Jules had everything she needed, Eve headed back downstairs and found Kane sitting on the couch. She walked over to him and leaned down, his face inches from hers. "Thank you," she whispered. "Thank you for calling Jules. Especially now."

"I knew you had to have been missing everyone, and I was happy that she could come down to support you." Eve got even closer and gave him a kiss on the lips.

"I'm so happy this is all hopefully ending soon."

"You and me both. I hope this puts a stop to any threats on your life. All I want to do is keep you safe and happy."

Eve moved forward once more and gave him another kiss on the lips before plopping down beside him on the couch. "There's one thing we don't know the answer to."

"And what's that?"

"There's no way that the Blakes could have done this on their own. Who put the tracking device on my car? Who almost hit me with the car in D.C.? Who was sending me those emails? Based on what we know, it would be too risky for a sitting congressman to do these things; he might get caught. So, I would assume that they hired someone to do the dirty work for them."

"It's funny that you're saying this because I was wondering the same thing. I'm waiting on an acquaintance to get back to me about that."

Eve leaned back with her eyes still on Kane. "Oh, really?"

"I have a hunch about who he might be, and I'm hoping they can prove me right."

"Well, are you going to give me any hints or just tell me who you think it is?" Eve could see that Kane was debating with himself about what to do. He took a deep breath before he began.

"Do you remember Sarah?"

"Sarah? Are you talking about Rae's old roommate?"

"Yes."

"What about her?"

"I'm pretty sure the same organization that hired her is the one that did all those things to you."

Eve couldn't stop her mouth from falling open. She stared at Kane for a few seconds, unable to process what he just said or to figure out what she wanted to say in response. When her brain could finally compute what he mentioned, she said, "What—why do you think it's them?"

"Well, Edwards, Holland, and Walker Consulting, also known as EHWC, is known in certain circles to be the premier company to go to when you want these types of things to happen. Whether it's tracking people or threatening people. So, they were already on my radar after what happened to Rae. There's also the fact that I'm sure they have a file on you because of any research that was done on Rae. It wouldn't be hard to continue gathering information as they wouldn't be starting from scratch."

"Well, do you think we can get them on this? Like I almost got hit by a car because of them."

Kane rubbed the back of his neck. "It would be hard to pin everything that happened to you on them, and that's just how they like it. That's what I'm waiting on my acquaintance to get back to me about. He might have any more information on that tracking device that was used on your car. Although it's very generic, he's digging around to see if there have been other instances where we have suspected that EHWC might have been involved in a case and that device was used. Like I said, this wouldn't explicitly tie them to what's going on with you, but it might give us something."

"Okay." Before she could utter another word, Jules walked down the stairs.

Jules smiled when she entered the living room, but that smile soon turned into a look of concern. Jules looked at Eve, then at Kane, then back to Eve. "What did I miss?"

26

———

The crowd was gathered in the event space and Eve could feel her nerves increasing tenfold, causing her body to vibrate. It felt like she was riding a roller coaster and about to go over the first bump. Kane must have sensed her nervous energy because, at that very moment, he placed an arm around her waist and pulled her into his side. She smiled at his reaction; he provided a sense of security that helped to restore some tranquility to her mind.

"Are you ready?"

Eve turned to Jules. "As ready as I'll ever be. This needs to end and we need to get a confession out of him. So much hurt and pain has been thrown around because of this and it needs to stop."

"Did you remember to send a message to you-know-who?"

Eve nodded. "I sent the message a few hours ago." They were referring to Abbie, who Eve had told she would be going public with everything she knew about Representative

Blake at this event. Abbie had wished her the best of luck but hadn't changed her mind about attending. Eve didn't say anything more because the host of the event took the stage.

While the host spoke, Eve shifted her feet, trying to find a comfortable position to stand in. It was a packed room, as everyone in Capitol and probably some neighboring towns came to watch Anthony Blake speak. Kane told her this had become a regular occurrence since they elected him.

"And now I want to welcome to the stage Representative Anthony Blake." The crowd gave a round of applause as he walked onto the stage, his bright smile showcasing the charisma of a seasoned politician, but Eve knew that, under this persona, was a deep dark secret. A secret that she was putting her neck on the line to expose.

The question-and-answer session started, and Eve, Kane, and Jules chose seats off to the side, near the front of the event hall. She noticed Kayla from Representative Blake's office was standing in the background talking to who Eve assumed was a coworker. Although Eve wanted to hightail it out of the venue due to nerves, she knew she had to sit here, let a couple of the questions be asked, and then spring her attack on him. He wasn't expecting her to be here, and she was confident in her ability to get him to admit what he did all those years ago.

"Maybe I should try to talk to him in private."

Kane looked at her through the corner of his eye. "After the mayor practically threatened you at the food drive, I don't think it's a good idea. This is probably your best bet. He won't be able to do anything besides deny and you have the facts to back it up."

Eve knew Kane was right. This was the best opportunity

for shock value. Plus, if the Blakes were behind the threats on her life, there is no way that they would give her an opportunity to question them in private again. Well, if they did, her safety would be at risk. Eve saw the person passing one of two microphones around the venue about to walk past her and she raised her hand so he noticed her. He dipped his head in acknowledgment and passed her the microphone. She waited until the person asking a question about safety in Capitol finished and the representative answered. When the host asked for the next question, Eve stood up.

"Speaking of safety, where were you on the evening that Abbie Henderson got hit by a car?"

A murmur passed over the crowd as they tried to figure out what was going on. Representative Blake gave Eve a skeptical look before he said, "I don't know what you're getting at."

"Where were you on the evening that Abbie got hit by a car?"

She could see the irritation building up in Anthony's body language. The clenching of Anthony's fists on the table. The way his eyes darted over the crowd. The slight paleness in his complexion that slowly morphed into a red.

"I don't remember exactly where I was that night. I mean, it's been what, fifteen years?"

"It's been eighteen years, Mr. Blake, and I don't think you've forgotten any of the details of that night, including how long ago it was. I also think it came up relatively recently, which is why some of your staff was talking about it." Eve spared a quick glance at Kayla and confirmed that Kayla knew she was talking about her.

Representative Blake stood up from his seat and approached the crowd, coming closer and closer to Eve. He turned his attention to the crowd and said, "Now you know none of this is true." He turned back to Eve and his face was stone cold serious.

"This is preposterous."

Mayor Blake appeared next to his son. His face turned a shade of red that Eve was sure that she had never seen on a human being before. Her gut told her that he might try to launch himself at her, but she didn't move an inch. Kane must have been thinking the same thing, because much like he did when she first met the mayor, Kane maneuvered his body toward hers, but he didn't push Eve behind him. Eve was grateful because she wanted to be the one that still had control over the situation versus him taking over.

"Ms. Jackson, do you know who I am? You have no proof of this, and I'm going to sue I you and the *Capitol Express*," sneered Representative Blake.

"I don't think you'll do any of that, Anthony."

Sounds of shock could be heard throughout the crowd and all attention was drawn to someone behind them.

Abbie Henderson stood a couple of feet away from Eve, and Eve sent her a small smile, assuring her that she was doing the right thing. "I'm tired of having to live a life where people don't know what really happened on that night eighteen years ago. And if no one believes me, so be it, but I'm ready to tell my truth right here, right now."

Eve watched a bunch of emotions appear on the congressman's face. He went from being surprised to angry in about two seconds flat. "This is all a lie! How dare you—"

"Anthony, you don't need to do this anymore. Just tell the truth. You hit me and while everyone thought the car just kept going, you didn't. You jumped out of your car almost immediately and checked on me before speeding off."

Anthony lunged at Eve but didn't get anywhere near her because of Kane's quick movements. By the time Kane had wrestled the congressman to the floor, Axel and his deputy appeared, helping to restrain Anthony and to get the panicked crowd under control. Once Kane was back by her side, he hugged her and she asked, "Are you okay?"

Kane nodded as his hands flew over her face, double-checking to make sure she was fine and safe. "I'm fine. He didn't touch me. Are you okay?"

"Yes."

"This whole thing is horseshit!" Representative Blake's exclamation stunned the crowd into silence. He lowered his voice as he strained against the handcuffs. "You both are going to pay for this."

"Didn't Abbie already pay enough? Especially when she wasn't at fault for any of this?"

Representative Blake growled but didn't say another word. With that, Axel escorted him out of the venue as the crowd looked on.

"Well, that was some action I wasn't expecting," Jules said once Eve, Kane, and she were sitting back at Kane's dining room table.

"Tell me about it," Eve said, resting her head on her arms.

"Jules, do you mind if I talk to Eve for a minute?"

Eve lifted her head back up and looked at Kane with an eyebrow raised.

"Sure. I'll go into the living room and watch TV."

Kane held his hand out and Eve accepted it before standing up from her chair. The energy she felt when his hand touched hers made her feel safe once more. He led her to the front door and closed it gently behind them once they were both outside. A light breeze welcomed them as Eve leaned on the railing in front of her.

"Eve, you did a spectacular job nailing Anthony up there."

"Thank you. I definitely feel a sense of relief now that it's over." She glanced at Kane before she continued, "I think it's over."

"My acquaintance confirmed that they found the same device used in several other cases that we think EHWC was involved in. But we have no concrete proof unless Anthony comes clean about that."

"And chances are he won't because who knows how much that would rock D.C.?"

Kane nodded before he continued, "That was just the first thing I wanted to tell you."

"What else did you want to say?"

Kane looked down at Eve and she could see some hesitation in his eyes. His normally clear hazel eyes, flecked with specs of gold, seemed stormy, almost as if he was unsure of what to say next.

"I wanted to talk to you about what you wanted to do about when we leave here. I assume you need to get back to D.C. sometime soon."

Eve sighed. "I do. With Blake's confession, I need to update my article, send it to Casey, and prepare for the interviews I need to give. I'm getting booked on cable news shows as we speak."

"Sounds like you're going to have a busy few weeks."

"I will, but that doesn't mean I won't make time for you."

Kane let out a nervous laugh. "Whew, I didn't know where this was going."

"Wait. Were you nervous? Kane Slade was nervous about what I would say?"

"All right, all right. Yes, I was nervous about what you would say regarding the future."

"Well, technically we haven't talked about what we wanted to do so..." Eve clasped her hands behind her back, rocked back and forth on her heels, and whistled.

"Eve, I don't want what we started here to end. I want to see where our relationship goes when we return to D.C."

"I. Do. Too." Eve stopped rocking on her heels and stood on her tiptoes to lay a kiss on Kane's lips, sealing the pledge to see where life took them, together.

EPILOGUE

"Kane, we have to leave soon." Eve said as she broke the kiss.

"But I haven't seen you all day."

Eve chuckled. "That's because we were both at work." Kane had come over to Eve's place after he finished working for the day and had barely given her an opportunity to open the door before his lips were on hers. She wouldn't have minded if they didn't have somewhere to be, but her desire to spend the evening in with him wasn't in the cards because they had some place to be in a few minutes.

"Such a shame, isn't it?" He said as he went back to trying to take her mind off of what they needed to do and where they needed to go. His lips migrated to her neck where he continued using his distraction techniques. They almost worked before Eve placed her hands on his chest and pushed him back gently.

She giggled before she said, "We have to leave in like two minutes because I refuse to be later than Rae and Flint. I wouldn't hear the end of it."

Kane's made a dramatic showing of looking at his left wrist, which was bare. "Then we have ninety seconds to continue this make-out session."

"How about we take a rain check and continue this when we get back? I need to put some more lip gloss on before we can go."

Kane's dramatics continued as he sighed. "I'm holding you to that rain check."

"I wouldn't expect anything else."

"I SWEAR, every time we come here, our group grows more."

Liv's comment made the group laugh uncontrollably. Everyone agreed to meet at the Green Hat for drinks and to chat, and Eve couldn't be happier. After spending several weeks away from D.C., she was so happy to be back with Kane and the rest of her friends. She placed a hand on Kane's knee, and she looked at him and smiled. He turned to look at her, still trying to contain his laughter.

"I love you." She whispered to him, her brown eyes staring into his hazel ones.

"I love you too." Kane leaned over and kissed Eve. Eve wrapped her arms around Kane to continue the kiss. The people and the noise around them faded into the background as Kane tried to deepened the kiss.

"Can't you guys... take this somewhere else?" Liv's interruption made Eve and Kane laugh before turning back to the table.

"We could, but we won't."

Liv rolled her eyes and shook her head but shot her friends a smile.

Eve and Kane had been back in D.C. for a few weeks now and things were going well. Representative Anthony Blake resigned and was dealing with the fallout of his actions from eighteen years ago. Eve suspected that he came clean only after he was forced to. He admitted that he did stop to check on Abbie before he sped off; he said ran to the nearest payphone and called 9-1-1. He claimed that it wasn't on purpose and that he had been messing around with the radio and wasn't paying attention to the road. Eve had doubts about his explanation and thought that it might have been tied to what Abbie overheard, but she didn't haven't any proof.

Kane's family was doing well and Capitol as a whole was dealing with the Blake family revelation pretty well. Abbie wasn't willing to admit what she had overheard from Mayor Blake a week before the accident, so Eve hadn't pushed. The plan was to keep that information under wraps unless she directed Eve to do something further.

Since Abbie had come forward at the former congressman's event, she had done several interviews about what she recalled about the night that had changed her life forever. This included an interview with Capitol's own *Independent Reporter*. It turned out that Mayor Blake had had a hand in making sure that several of the articles about the car accident weren't included on the newspaper's website. That had all been rectified and the *Independent Record* was one of the first newspapers to ask for an interview.

Mayor Blake went on a leave of absence Eve assumed had to do with history finally catching up with his son. Eve would be shocked if he would keep his position and not be run out of town.

Eve and Kane glanced down at his phone when it lit up on the table. He read the notification before looking over at her. He leant over to whisper in her ear. "That was Hensley texting me asking when we were coming back into town."

Eve smiled. She wasn't surprised that Hensley had messaged Kane. She had reached out to Eve last week about the couple returning to Capitol and Eve told her she didn't know when they would be back, but would follow up with Kane. Clearly Hensley had grown impatient.

Before the couple could discuss the text further, a voice drew their attention away from Kane's phone.

"Hey, you guys."

Eve turned to the sound of the voice and saw Rae, Flint, and another man standing in front of them. He looked vaguely familiar, but she couldn't place him. Her eyes shifted between Flint and the stranger, and she noted some similarities. She leaned over and whispered to Kane, "Why does he look familiar?"

"That's Garrett."

The information clicked immediately. All of the things Kane told her about Knox flowed back. She heard Jules gasp. Eve turned to look at her friend Jules, because she knew that their history was rocky, but couldn't read her face.

"Guys, we hope it's all right that we brought Garrett with us. He's moving back to the area, and we figured it didn't hurt for him to be out of the house."

"Literally. I'm staying with them until my new apartment is ready at the end of the month. Easier than living with Mom and Dad though."

The group laughed, and Eve's eyes didn't leave Jules. She sat up straighter and threw her long blonde hair over her shoulder. A smile appeared on her face. And that smile was faker than a three-dollar bill.

Eve watched as Flint introduced his brother to everyone at the table with a smile, and when he got to Jules, she watched the smirk form on his face.

"It's a pleasure to see you again, Jules."

"I do not return the pleasure, Garrett."

Eve leaned over and whispered to Kane, "The gist I get is that Jules was close childhood friends with Flint and Garrett's twin sisters, and she never gotten along with Garrett. He went away to college and stayed away... until now."

Kane nodded. "I've met Garrett before but didn't know his history with Jules."

"I don't even know the half of it, but this might get interesting with him being back in town."

Eve looked back at Jules, whose glare was fixed on Garrett. This might get interesting indeed.

SNEAK PEEK AT BETRAYAL IN THE CAPITOL

"Dad, is everything okay?" Jules Cartwright gently closed the door to her father's office. He sat there with his head in his hands. She heard the yelling coming from his office and it took everything in her to not run in to find out what was wrong.

"Hi, sweetheart. Anything you need?"

"No, I was just coming in to check on you. I heard a lot of yelling coming from in here."

"It was nothing. What are you still doing here anyway?"

Jules was no fool, and she noticed that he deflected the conversation.

"I was wrapping up a few things before I head out. Are you sure you don't need anything?"

"I'm sure." William Cartwright stood up from his massive desk and walked toward his daughter. She stepped into her father's embrace and visions of how he used to do this when she was younger flashed through her mind. Now she felt like the roles were reversed.

"Tell Mom I said hello."

He placed a quick kiss on her head. "Will do. Don't forget she wants you to come over for dinner this weekend."

"I know and I'll be there. See you then."

Jules stepped back and smiled before turning around and walking out of her dad's office and back to her own. She flipped her blonde hair over one shoulder and grabbed her jacket and purse before closing her work laptop. She checked her phone and saw that she had a message from Rae.

Rae: Hey, could you stop by my house on your way home from work? If you're busy, we can chat over the phone.

Jules: I don't have any fundraisers tonight, so I'm happy to stop by.

Jules's office was less than ten minutes away from Rae and Flint's new home, and her apartment was about five minutes away from them. She hit the switch, turning off the lights, and headed toward the elevators. Once she was down in the lobby, she walked outside and made her way to Rae's home. When she was near the driveway, Rae opened the front door.

"Hey, I'm so sorry I invited you over on such short notice. I have wine if that is any consolation."

"It's not a problem and I'm always down for some wine."

"Down? Stop hanging around Liv, okay?" Rae said with a laugh, backing up to let Jules pass her.

"So, what's up?" Jules said, taking her jacket off and giving it to Rae, who was waiting for it. "Every time I come over here, it looks even more beautiful."

"Thanks! It's coming together." Rae and Flint had been in their new place for a few months and Rae still claimed that they were slowly making the place homier—between Flint's busy congressional schedule and Rae's work schedule.

"Is Flint home?" Jules intentionally didn't mention the

other person she knew was staying with them because she couldn't stand him.

"He's not, and neither is Garrett." Rae looked at her, raising her eyebrow before going to retrieve the wine. Garrett, Flint's brother, had been staying with them for the last couple of weeks because he was waiting on his apartment to be ready.

"I didn't mention him on purpose."

"I know you didn't, but I was teasing you. Anyway, I invited you over because I missed you and wanted to hang out with you. Also, I was wondering if there might be a possibility for the Cartwright Foundation to team up with Wild Parks, Wild Lands to put together a gala to support environmental initiatives."

Jules took a sip of her wine; the liquid felt delicious going down her throat. "I have little control over that because I'm on the communications team, but I can let my dad know to see if he would be game for it."

"Great! Enough work talk, let's talk about some gossip. What the heck is up with you and Garrett?"

"Honey, I'm home!" Rae laughed when she heard her fiancé come in the door. She jumped up and ran over to Flint, laying a kiss on his lips. Jules rolled her eyes at the person behind them. With a smirk, Garrett took off his suit jacket without taking his eyes off of Jules.

"Of course you'd be here."

"I'm staying here, so none of that is surprising. You, on the other hand, I didn't expect."

That makes two of us.

Pre-order Betrayal in the Capitol Today!

ABOUT THE AUTHOR

B. Ivy Woods has been writing for as long as she can remember. After getting her Bachelor of Arts in Political Science and Environmental Policy and a Master's in Energy Policy and Law degree and working in the environmental field for several years, she decided to become a stay-at-home mom. That is when thoughts of a writing career really took off. Although she competed in NaNoWriMo multiple times, 2019 was the first year that she won. This win inspired her to make writing a career. Her debut novel was self-published in 2020.

Although she is originally from New York City, she currently lives in the DMV (Washington, D.C., Maryland, Virginia) with her husband, daughter, dog, and cat.

www.bivywoods.com